Marilyn the Wild

BOOKS BY JEROME CHARYN

Once Upon A Droshky (1964)
On The Darkening Green (1965)
The Man Who Grew Younger (1967)
Going To Jerusalem (1967)
American Scrapbook (1969)
Eisenhower, My Eisenhower (1971)
The Tar Baby (1973)
Blue Eyes (1975)
Marilyn the Wild (1976)

Marilyn the Wild

A NOVEL

Jerome Charyn

ARBOR HOUSE
NEW YORK

Library of Congress Catalogue Card Number: 76-31072

ISBN: 0-87795-129-2

Manufactured in the United States of America

For Hy Cohen

Part One

1.

———————————

"BLUE Eyes."

She was indebted to the gouges in his face, high cheeks that could blunt a scary color. The specks in his eyes might harm any girl who had just run away from her husband. She didn't want to be snared again. She had come to him for Russian tea, firm pillows, and the comforts of a temporary home.

"Marilyn," he said, with a nasalness that made her twitch. He had her father's voice. And she refused to wrestle with Isaac on Coen's bed.

"Marilyn, shouldn't you talk to Isaac?"

"Screw him." She had unpacked an hour ago. Her suitcase was under Coen's laundry bag. She intended to mingle her dirty underwear with his. She would rinse them in the bathtub together, with the Woolite she had brought, after Coen went to work.

11

"Marilyn, suppose he finds out? I'm not too good at lying."

She held his collarbone in her teeth, made perfect little bites that were meant to arouse her father's man. She would tolerate no protests from him. She dug her nipples into his chest. She worked spit under his arm. But she'd trap herself, fall victim to Coen, if she couldn't get around his eyes.

Whenever she weakened and let his infernal blue peek out at her, she would lower her head to lick the scars on his back (souvenirs Coen had acquired in the street), or stare at the holster on his desk.

She straddled him, rubbing his prick with a wet finger. The blueness couldn't hurt her now. Coen's eyes were thickening with impure spots. She pushed Coen inside herself, milked him with the pressure off her thighs, until she lost all sense of Isaac, and that husband of hers, a Brooklyn architect, and responded to Coen's gentle body.

Twice divorced at twenty-five, she could chew up husbands faster than any other Bronx-Manhattan girl who had bombed out of Sarah Lawrence. Isaac had always been there to find husbands for her, genteel men with forty-thousand-dollar jobs and a flush of college degrees. Her father sat at Headquarters behind the paneled walls of the First Deputy Police Commissioner. He'd been invited to Paris, she heard, as the World's Greatest Cop (of 1970–71), or something close to that. And Coen was Isaac's fool, a spy attached to the First Dep.

She gulped through her nose, smelling Coen's blond hairs. She came five times, her tongue twisting deeper into her mouth. She could beg him now.

"Come in me, Manfred, please."

She saw the hesitation in the pull of his lip. He was frightened of knocking up Isaac's girl, and imposing a grandchild on his Chief, a baby Coen. But Marilyn was a stubborn creature. She soothed the bumps in Coen's jaw with the side of her face. She understood the depths of her father's cop. He was a shy boy, a Jewish orphan with a handsome streak that fed itself on Bronx sadnesses: both his parents were suicides. She softened the points of tension in his throat with the flesh of her shoulder and the powerful membranes in her ear.

Marilyn hadn't reckoned on the telephone. Coen was out of her before she could kick the receiver under the bed. "Fuck" was all she could think to say.

She crouched against Coen so she could listen to her father. He was calling from Times Square. "Manfred," he croaked, "Marilyn's left her husband again. Has she been in touch with you?"

"No," Blue Eyes said. Marilyn was grateful that he didn't lose his erection under duress from her father.

"Stay put," Isaac said. "She always comes to you."

Coen returned to bed without a prick. Marilyn couldn't hold a grudge against the cop. Her father had half of New York City by the balls.

"Isaac's smart," she said. "He's got me mapped in his head like a Monopoly board. He knows all my resting places, that father of mine. Every water hole."

"Don't goose him too hard, Marilyn. He worries about you."

"Wake up, Manfred. You're just like me. We're on Isaac's casualty list. Aren't both of us divorcees?"

And she made the cop laugh. She'd fall in love with him, maybe, if he had the nerve to crumple his shield and spit in Isaac's face. But she shouldn't be harsh with him, strangle him with fantasies and expectations. Coen was Coen.

❖

Isaac hadn't been cruising Times Square, nesting in ratty bars, peeking into pornographers' windows, for the First Deputy's office. He was on a personal mission. He pushed in and out of his car with a photograph in his fist. He had the First Deputy's private sedan at his disposal, a big Buick with bullet-proof windows. But he wouldn't use the First Dep's chauffeur. Isaac had his own man. Fat Brodsky, a first-grade detective with piggly eyes, was Isaac's toad.

"Who's the girlie, Isaac? You say you haven't seen her since she was five. How are you gonna recognize her from a dumb photograph?"

"Never mind," Isaac said. He found a girl with a thick nose and a high, summer skirt (it was February) near Forty-sixth Street. He opened the door for her. "Honey Schapiro, get in."

The girl had welts on her exposed kneecaps. She growled at Isaac. "I'm Naomi, Mister. Who are you?"

He lunged at her and installed her on his lap, but he couldn't shut the door. Honey was kicking too hard. Isaac had to keep her from biting his ears.

"What is this? You don't belong to the pussy posse? I know all them guys."

She began screaming for her protector, a dude named Ralph, who rushed over from Forty-fifth Street in his leather coat. Brodsky upset him more than Isaac. The chauffeur was pointing a holster at Ralph's groin.

"Hey brother," Ralph said, with a nod for Isaac. "Speak to me." Ralph didn't reach for his money clip. The Buick made him cautious; ordinary house bulls wouldn't have come to him in so conspicuous a car.

"You bringing her down?"

"No," Isaac said. "She's going home to her father."

"Cut the shit, man. You asking me to buy you a hat? I'll buy, but I ain't supplying the feather. Fifty is all I'm giving today." Then he saw the blue teeth on Isaac's badge. He shuddered under his coat. Ralph was wise to the nitty-gritty of Manhattan stationhouses: no detective carried a badge with blue teeth.

Isaac spoke through his window. "Forget about Honey Schapiro, you understand? If I catch her above Fourteenth Street again, I'll personally break your face." He signaled to Brodsky, and Ralph waved goodbye to the Buick on jiggling knees. He didn't like to be swindled. If he'd known how Honey was connected, he wouldn't have battered her legs. He'd have rewarded her with a better corner, and a cleaner clientele. That ugly Jew broad had her hooks into the police.

Brodsky laughed on the ride downtown with Isaac and the girl. "Boy, you can scare nigger pimps. Isaac, did you look at his eyes?"

"Shut up," Isaac said. And Brodsky was satisfied. He loved to be scolded by his Chief. A slur from Isaac made him vigorous and alert. Brodsky could have farted on every cop at Headquarters, including the number one Irisher, First Deputy O'Roarke. The chauffeur swore himself to Isaac. Isn't he going to Paris, France, Brodsky reasoned. What other cop travels four thousand miles for a lecture?

The girl moved off Isaac's lap. She panicked at the benches and frozen grass of Union Square park. Second Avenue curled her chin into the padding under the window. With glum, bitter cheeks she watched Isaac's descent into the lower East Side.

Brodsky became aware of the girl's worsening state. "Honey, would you like a gumdrop?"

"Leave her alone," Isaac said.

They parked in a lot behind the Essex Street housing project, Isaac sticking his Deputy Chief Inspector's card over the dashboard. The smell of urine accompanied them to the back doors of the project. Brodsky was about to comment on the smell when he noticed Isaac's glare. He displayed his badge to the housing guard, who had a disfigured nightstick and stubble on his face. He read the graffiti in the elevator car with obvious contempt. Essex Street had the musk and corrosive charm of a zoo. Brodsky lived in a house on Spuyten Duyvil hill. He came to Essex, Clinton, and Delancey to buy horseradish and squares of onion bread that were unknown in his section of Riverdale.

Isaac and the girl lost their winter flush in the overheated halls of the ninth floor. They drifted into an apartment with mousy green walls. Brodsky was the last one inside. A man in silk pajamas, without a tooth in his face, hugged the girl and cried into his sleeve. Sensing Brodsky, a stranger to him, he recovered himself. "Isaac, I search for months, and you find her in an hour and a half. You're a magician, Isaac. She was a baby the last time you saw her."

"I had her picture, Mordecai. It was nothing."

"Nothing he says. The police force would be poking in a ditch without you."

"Mordecai, I have to go." The Chief kept his eyes on Honey; she couldn't relax in her father's grip. She had the waxy features of a bloated doll.

"Isaac, one more thing. Philip is looking for you."

Isaac headed for the door; he didn't want to be sucked into another family dispute. He had his own troubles: a wild, uncontrollable daughter who shed husbands in the middle of winter.

"I'll catch him later, Mordecai. Not now."

Brodsky climbed into the elevator with Isaac. He could hear shouts and cries coming from the apartment, and the echoes of a slap. He smiled at the tumult raised by Mordecai and Honey. The Chief jabbed him with a thumb. "Brodsky, put your mind somewhere else. That's private business."

"Isaac, who is that guy? Your mother's boyfriend, or what?"

"I went to high school with him."

"You're kidding me. Isaac, he could be your grandfather, I swear."

"Forget about it. Mordecai doesn't have a Park Avenue dentist to look after his gums."

"Isaac, what's his trade?"

"Mordecai? He's a leftover from World War Two. He minded all the Victory gardens from Chinatown to Corlears Hook, but he didn't save a carrot for himself."

What could Isaac tell his chauffeur? Mordecai squatted down a hundred yards from his high school, Seward Park, and never stirred. Isaac had nothing against fixed perimeters. He was born on West Broadway, in a block owned by London Jews, men and women who had a more powerful vocabulary than their Yankee neighbors. Yet he preferred Essex Street, where his mother kept a junk shop, to the London Jews of West Broadway, or the Riverdale of Brodsky and Kathleen, Isaac's estranged wife.

The chauffeur stopped at the pickle factory on Essex and

Broome for a jar of grated horseradish roots, pure and white, without the sweetening effect of red beets. Only dehydrated women and quiffs from the District Attorney's office would buy red horseradish. He put his nose in the jar, sniffed until his eyes went blind, and recovered in time to watch Isaac pass Sophie Sidel's junk shop.

"Isaac, aren't you going to sit with your mother?"

The Chief wouldn't answer. "Brodsky, the First Dep needs his car. Bring it to him."

Isaac was hoping to skirt away from his mother. He had too many unexplainable items in his head. He'd visit her after Paris, not before. He went into Hubert's delicatessen, five doors up from Sophie's. The place seemed in perfect order, with fish balls steaming the counter glass, and the juice of several puddings bubbling down off the stove, but Hubert himself was in disarray. A little man, with pointy shoulders and a lion's shaggy scalp, he had lumps on his brow and pieces of toilet paper covering dark spots along his chin.

"Hubert, what's wrong?" Isaac said, occupying his favorite chair. "Did you shave with one eye this morning?" Isaac couldn't have anticipated any evil. The delicatessen was his roost. Other Deputy Chief Inspectors sat in the chosen clam-houses of Mulberry and Grand, elbows away from Mafia lieutenants and princelings. But Isaac ate alone. At Hubert's he could follow the cracks in the wall without interruptions. Hubert hadn't lost a dime from his cash register in fifteen years. East Side pistols learned to steer south of the delicatessen by habit. If they did come inside Hubert's, to warm their hands over a cup of winter tea, they made sure to leave an elaborate tip.

The Chief wasn't insensitive. When that big lion's head

didn't come back at him with a pout, and splash barley soup on the tablecloth with customary verve, Isaac took a different turn.

"Who did it to you? Were they white or black?"

"White as snow," Hubert said.

"How much did they take?"

"Nothing. They didn't touch the register. They broke a few chairs, slapped me, and left."

"Hubert, what did they wear?"

"Army coats, navy coats, who remembers? Their faces were covered up. With ski masks."

"Then how can you be sure they were white?"

"By their hands, Isaac. By their hands. One of them was a girl. I'm no detective, but I can tell the outline of a tit."

"When did it happen?"

"Yesterday. Just before closing."

"How come it takes a whole day for me to hear about it?"

"Isaac, close the inquisition, please. It isn't a police matter. Crazy kids. They could have picked on anybody."

"Absolutely," Isaac said, with a thickened tongue. "They were playing trick-or-treat. Only Halloween doesn't come in February. Your cash was too good for them. So they took their profits on your skull. How many of them were there?"

"There were three." Hubert's mouth was crammed with spit.

"I'll be gone for a week. My man will look into it."

The lumps grew dark on the lion's head. "Isaac, I don't want a bully in my store. Brodsky has wide elbows. He doesn't give a person room to drink his soup."

"I'll send you Coen. He's small. He'll charm your customers to sleep with his blue eyes."

Isaac knocked in the window of the dairy restaurant on Ludlow Street; it was a place he liked to avoid. It was crammed with hungry playwrights and scholars who tried to tangle Isaac into conversations about Spinoza, Israel, police brutality, and the strange brotherhood of Aaron and Moses. The playwrights weren't scornful of him. They recognized Isaac as the patron saint of Ludlow and East Broadway. He kept bandits off their streets, but his strength was no surprise to them. He'd been suckled on strange milk. His mother was a woman with an obstinate heart. She befriended Arabs and Puerto Ricans over Jews.

They laughed at the reaction of the cashier lady to Isaac's knock. Ida Stutz threw off her uniform and smacked powder on her face. This one was Isaac's fiancée. They knew Isaac had an Irish wife up in Riverdale, but it would have been unwise of them to offend Ida. She furnished the scholars with toothpicks, sneaked them pats of butter and extra rolls, because she had a kindness for undernourished men. Ida was a girl with ample arms and legs. Whatever prettiness she had came from such proportions. She made her own lunch hours at the Ludlow restaurant. She was a dray horse most mornings and afternoons. The owners of the restaurant worked her silly. They could count on Ida's sweat, and Ida's husky back. So they allowed her one oddity. When the Chief knocked, Ida disappeared.

Isaac kept two stunted rooms on Rivington Street. He had to share a toilet with an ancient bachelor who peed wantonly.

He washed his body in a kitchen tub that couldn't accommodate all of Isaac until his ears crept between his knees. It was in this undignified position that Ida found the Chief. She saw his suitcase on the bed, burgeoning with starched underwear, notebooks, and unbleached honey.

"Isaac, I know you. Soaping your belly is just a blind. Your brains are already in Paris."

Squirming in the tub, a prisoner to his own knees, Isaac had to smile. His wife Kathleen had been an extraordinary beauty. Even at forty-nine (she was five years older than the Chief), she had bosoms that could make Ida blush. But Isaac had never been a connoisseur of flesh. He gave up his home in Riverdale because Kathleen had grown independent of him. She was a woman with spectacular real estate. She had properties in Florida that ate up most of her energy. Isaac didn't have to crawl to the lower East Side for love. He could have stayed uptown with handsome widows, starlets who were hungry for intellectual cops, or bimbos with penthouses and rebuilt behinds. Ida pleased him more. She had a tongue that could scold him properly, and a mouth that could suck up all his teeth. It didn't matter to her how Isaac behaved. Ida wasn't fragile. She could match the Chief in kisses, bear hugs, and bites. She began to undress.

"This is your last bath in America. Aren't you sorry you don't have a bigger tub?"

"Ida, there's a tub at Headquarters that could fit you, me, and five more cops. Should we go?"

"We'll go," she said. "When you're not in a rush." And she dried him with Florentine talc from Mulberry Street, a powder so fine that it could cure the most subtle rash. She lay on the bed near Isaac's sweetened body, without bothering

21

to push the suitcase aside. His bull neck, evenly talced, couldn't intimidate her. Ida didn't suffer from delusions about her fiancé. He had torn out the eye of a bandit from East New York, broken the arms of suspicious characters, survived gunfights with Puerto Ricans and hardened Jews. But she'd seen the infant inside the bear. He was a man who loved to be babied. Under the talcumed skin was a dread that Ida knew how to smother. The Chief made no pretense of masculinity. He shuddered in Ida's arms. His passions were the primitive clutch of a drowning man.

The bear was quiet after loving her. Ida wouldn't give in to his sulkiness while she dripped with Isaac's sperm. So she pulled his nose. The Chief kicked one leg over the honey jar and a stack of underpants.

"Where are your troubles coming from, Isaac?"

"Ah," he lied. "I was thinking of a case." He mumbled Hubert's name. "A gang beat him up. They didn't touch the register. It sounds flukey to me."

"They're probably rejects from the Jewish Defense League. Maybe Hubert isn't kosher enough. He serves butter with meat."

"Don't, Ida. That's not the work of Jewish kids. Giving an old man puffs on his head."

"You think that's special? Look at my arms."

He glanced at the bruises on Ida's flesh, thumbprints turning brown. The halo surrounding each bruise told him the pressure that must have been applied.

"Same gang," she said. "They visited me too. They stole blintzes, not money."

"Ida, what else did they do?"

"Little stunts. One of them grabs my arms, while the other sticks a hand in my blouse."

The Chief scattered underwear off his bed.

"Ida, I'll find that hand and chop it off when I get back."

With two fingers Ida straightened the curl in his lip. "Should I tell you the number of times a customer has tried to grab a handful of me?"

"These weren't customers," the Chief said. But Ida had him by the ears. She was massaging the tiny bones at the back of his head. Isaac should have been putting on his tie. He didn't have ten minutes to spare. His face was deep in Ida's chest. The suitcase fell.

Isaac couldn't wrestle free of old questions. Ida's milky smell brought Marilyn home to him. The Chief wasn't playing incest on his bed. He didn't confuse the girls. But kisses could hurt. He was coveting Ida's milk, when he had a daughter who went from husband to husband, and couldn't confide in him.

2.

————————————

Marilyn survived on lumps of tuna fish. She didn't peek about until Blue Eyes could assure her that Isaac was on the plane for Paris. The First Dep's office had verified the news: Isaac embarked at 7 P.M. She'd been lazing with Coen since noon. She watched him button his pretty neck into the collar of a white shirt. The holster went on last. "Manfred, wait. I'm going with you."

Coen was minding Isaac's car. Blue Eyes hated to drive. There were too many stirrings in doorways, beggars jumping into the street, dogs chasing buses or crawling under his wheels, old women losing their memories in the middle of the road, to thwart a cop's eye.

"You suppose Isaac is going to revise the entire French police?" Marilyn was bored. She couldn't get Coen to jabber. So she enticed him with her father's secrets. "Manfred, you have a tricky boss. He won't be mingling with detectives over there. Isaac went to visit his father."

Lines formed on Coen's chin. Marilyn was ashamed of her crude tactics. Coen's father had killed himself. Ten years ago, while Blue Eyes was stationed in Germany, Papa Coen decided to take gas. Coen wore his sad face ever since.

"I didn't know Isaac had a father . . . a father that's alive."

"It's an embarrassment to him. Like having a brother in jail."

Coen had learned not to mention Isaac's baby brother Leo, who was entombed in Crosby Street, in a temporary annex to the old Civil Jail, because of alimony trouble. The Police Department shrugged at this indignity to itself. But the First Dep was powerless. Leo refused to step out of jail.

"Marilyn, what's embarrassing about a father?"

"He deserted the family years ago. Isaac had to leave school. Didn't he tell you? His father was once a millionaire. Joel Sidel, the fur-collar prince. He threw it over for a stinking paint brush. He had a long nose, like Gauguin. He thought Paris was the new Tahiti. He wanted to paint the jungles around Sacré Coeur."

Jungles in Paris meant nothing to Coen. "Why did Isaac pick now for a visit?"

"Because he's had intimations of mortality." Coen's starved cheeks made her sorrowful of her rotten vocabulary, fed at Sarah Lawrence and at the dinner tables of her many husbands. "Manfred, he's going on forty-five. That's a dangerous age. Isaac needs his father. Seeing Joel will prove to him that he's got years to go."

Coen dropped her at Crosby Street. He would park in Isaac's slot at the police garage, march into Headquarters, blow dust off Isaac's desk, and answer phone calls in the name of his Chief. He would say, "First Deputy's office, Inspector Sidel," with Marilyn's perfume ripening on him.

It was past official visiting hours at the Crosby Street annex, but Marilyn had no difficulty getting in. None of the guards could recollect the name of her current husband. They knew her as "Miss Sidel." Not even the deputy warden was willing to tamper with Isaac's girl. He brought Leo out to her himself, mumbling little flatteries about Isaac's trip. "He'll teach Paris how to nab their crooks. You can bet on that, Miss Sidel."

Leo was floundering in an oversized prison shirt. It was hard to consider him an uncle. He'd be Isaac's baby brother for life.

Leo was devoid of prison scars. He set his own hours at Crosby Street, ate candy out of a machine, destroyed the guards in pinochle, checkers, and bridge. There were no criminals to mingle with. Just cases like Leo, men who had faulted on their alimony, and were being held in civil contempt. Detectives from the Sheriff's office had swiped Leo out of a congested lobby in the building where he worked, exposing him to the shameful stare of executives, buyers, and girls from the typing pool, and led him away in handcuffs, on a complaint from his former wife. The Sheriff's detectives were as restless as Leo. It made them miserable to be recognized as the men who had collared the brother of Isaac the Just.

Marilyn had a softness for Leo. She hadn't come to him as Isaac's compassionate daughter. She could identify with Leo's plight. Leo was her special kinsman: both of them had endured busted marriages, both of them had been skinned alive. They could hug and kiss in the prison's reception room

27

without one snarl from the guards. "Marilyn, are you laughing same as me? I can breathe. The word has come down that Isaac is out of the country. I'll grow fat in the next few days. What about you?"

Marilyn extended the hug.

"Uncle Leo, I wish I had three thousand to get you out of here. Would that be enough to satisfy stupid Selma? I'd strangle her for you, if you want. Don't you think Isaac could spring me? Only that would leave you a widower with kids. Have Davey and Michael come to visit you?"

Leo grew somber in the reception room. He broke away from Marilyn. "They stick with their mother," he said. "They send me poison notes. Selma forces them to practice their penmanship on me. I can hear her tongue behind the words. 'Dad, you're killing us.' Marilyn, that woman has the money to choke an elephant. She keeps her bankbooks in an old brassiere."

Marilyn chafed at her inability to help Leo. Her last two husbands had been rich, but she was left a pauper. She had to borrow money from Coen.

"Sophie or Isaac would put up the till. Leo, I could ask."

"Never. Marilyn, don't forget. In October I was forty-two. Can I go begging to my mother, or scrounge from big Isaac? Better they should take me out and shoot me. I don't care how they finish me off. As long as Sophie doesn't know. Marilyn, Isaac didn't tell mama, did he? I call her every morning. I say I'm at a hotel that doesn't have a phone in the room. Funny, she didn't answer today. She must be out buying more junk."

"Isaac fucks over everybody, but he won't snitch. Not because of you. It would make him too uncomfortable. He'd have to explain to your mother why you're sitting in a jail.

Leo, don't fidget. I'll convince Sophie for you. I'm going there right now."

The guards groped for banalities on the way out. They were fishing to stay on Isaac's good side. "We'll watch Leo, Miss Sidel. We've made it like a country club for him."

Marilyn crossed the Bowery into Isaac's territories: the Puerto Rican–Jewish East Side. She had to smile at the old Forsyth Street synagogue, now a "Templo Adventista," with its Star of David still intact in the little circular window near the roof. Later she would shop for underpants on Orchard Street. She had to see Sophie first.

Israel had taken over Essex Street. Apricots from Galilee, Haifa plums, and spaghetti made in Tel Aviv dominated the windows of tiny groceries. She realized what a blight this must be for her grandmother, who championed the Diaspora, homeless Arabs and Jews in a Gentile universe. Sophie didn't have the usual allotment of junk on parade outside her door. Was she feeding soup to hobos? Or feeling up a plump goose at the Christian butcher? The door was ajar.

Marilyn had no knowledge of Haifa plums. She was a girl with an Irish nose, a captive of churches on Marble Hill, with memories of communion gloves and priests who dribbled spit. Hot-blooded, she allowed her cherry to be swiped at twelve and a half. Past fourteen, her fame extended from Riverdale to Washington Heights, with pieces off her underpants rotting in the cellars of Fordham Road. Uptown precociousness couldn't connect a girl to her mysterious grandmother, Sophie the Hoarder. So Marilyn interpreted the lay of things. Sophie wouldn't spite her own wares to give her affections to a hobo. She was more careful than that. Marilyn stepped over the damaged perambulators that Sophie prized. They were hopeless vehicles. None of them could move. But Sophie had trussed their bodies with great lengths of wire.

Marilyn ventured deeper into the shop. Torn lampshades couldn't trouble her. That might have been Sophie's doing. She peeked under a mound of blankets with odd lumps in a corner. She wasn't shocked by Sophie's arm; it rested in a natural position, without a flaw in the beautiful veins. Was this how a grandmother sleeps?

Marilyn tugged at the blankets, following the course of that arm. Sophie's head emerged, lying in blood that had turned to a thick, corrosive jelly. The jelly reached to her ears. She had marks on her forehead that resembled the sink of a belt buckle into skin. Marilyn's screams came in a dry wisp. She shambled towards the telephone. She didn't consider ambulances. In her panic she could only think of dialing for Coen.

3.

Isaac sat in a damp palace high on the Quai Voltaire. His feet were cold. Surrounded by gunsmiths, retired police inspectors, manufacturers of snooping devices, and a team of specialists from the crime labs of Antwerp and Bruges, he tried to make do with his high-school French. Sentences galloped in his ear. He couldn't decipher all the sputter. Isaac was miserable at heart. His first walk in Paris had broken him.

Armored with New York, he came swollen-eyed, ready to lick his honey jar and scorn this town. Isaac had no instinct for sightseeing. He wasn't the sort of man who could gravitate towards the Eiffel Tower and the Champ de Mars. A few months back, Herbert Pimloe, the Harvard boy, an underchief with the First Deputy's office, and a voracious traveler, had returned home from Paris with a newspaper clipping for Isaac, which advertised a certain Monsieur Sidel, Portraitiste, with permanent headquarters in the lobby of an avenue Kléber hotel, near the Arc de Triomphe. "Chief," Pimloe said, with a finger on the clipping, and proud of himself. "Could that be a relative of yours?" Isaac had a burn in his throat. He hadn't expected his father to play Lazarus after twenty-five years. Joel Sidel was supposed to be among the missing and the dead. Isaac had wanted to forget his father's name. Now he thought of murdering Joel, or confronting him on the avenue Kléber, and bruising his head. Isaac schemed and scratched a little. He invited himself to a conference on crime staged for gunsmiths and provincial detectives. He was in Paris to kill, maim, and collect his due.

On his way to the conference, crossing the Seine, Isaac was prepared to spit at barges in the river, ignore shrill parrots belonging to old women with dust on their clothes, and avoid bookstalls and organ grinders. But he couldn't guard himself properly against the Ile de la Cité. A stone island, a medieval city that rose out of the water, it turned Isaac dumb. He stared at the island's grassy point, a twitch of green in front of gray mansion walls and the tips of Notre Dame. Stone pushing through the blur of a smoking river was insufferable to Isaac. Nothing in New York could swallow up this kind of vision. The chimneys of Welfare Island were piddling things compared to such damp walls. Isaac arrived at the conference with a scowling face.

One of the specialists from Bruges cornered Isaac after a short address on Parisian bank robbers. The Flemish man, who spoke a powerful English, made pessimistic swipes with his head that Isaac failed to comprehend. "Inspector Sidel, what is the position in America? Do you have amateurs committing crimes? Disgusting little apaches who are impossible to trace? Paris is flooded with them. I don't mean the scum of the African quarters. They're no threat to us. But young savages from the government projects around Clignancourt, and the other little holes at the ends of Paris—cockroaches with pistols in their hands. These roaches appear on the Champs-Elysées, stick up a bank, and crawl into their holes. What can one do? No grid, no organized gang, no strict underworld. Nothing but roaches, isolated roaches."

"We have them in the United States, Monsieur, but not so many," Isaac said, preoccupied with the painter Joel, his recreant father at the avenue Kléber hotel.

"Then what advice do you have for our friends in Paris, Inspector Sidel?"

"Go into the projects."

"With an army?"

"No, with spies."

"Ah," the Flemish man said, warming to Isaac. "It's a matter of infiltration. If you can't flush out the roaches, you sleep in their beds. Inspector, stay in Paris. You have a future with the Sûreté.

Isaac abandoned the conference before lunch. He regained his stride on the Quai Voltaire, walking towards the Invalides. He would be fine so long as he could distance himself from the sweating stones of the Cité. New York crept back to him; the Mansard roofs of Commerce Street, the crumbling walls of Cherry Lane, the slaughterhouses at Gansevoort, the incredible steel-shuttered factories of Lafayette and upper Mulberry. He could take Paris in a wink.

The boulevards above the Trocadero were welcome ground to Isaac. He didn't have to deal with crooked streets. He could close his eyes and sniff out Madison Avenue in the little bakeries and jewelry shops off the rue Hamelin. He wasn't astounded by The Iroquois of avenue Kléber: it had to be a hotel for rich Americans. All the tributaries of the Ohio snarled over Isaac's ears from a huge pictograph on the front wall. He had to go around an enormous Eiffel Tower in the center of The Iroquois. Isaac refused to smile.

He had his father at a disadvantage. Joel Sidel was the only painter in the lobby. Isaac couldn't be compassionate to the easel of a seventy-year-old. This was the man who had turned his mother crazy, and made a weakling of his brother. Sophie blundered into a rag shop, Isaac became a *flic*, and Leo drifted from boyhood to marriage to alimony jail.

Isaac couldn't ignore his father's technique. Joel snared Americans off the elevators; with a wag of his finger and artful hunchings of his back he would lure a couple over to his bench. While husband and wife posed with camera, light meter, and guide books, Joel dipped his fat brush into a can and painted their outline and obvious features in under a minute, before they had a chance to protest. He charged twenty francs for his work. Verisimilitude didn't count. The couples would have been offended by too much accuracy. They were in awe of Joel's speed with a brush. Isaac grunted into the lapels of his raincoat. He hadn't come to Paris to play spy.

Joel wasn't asleep. He made a primal recognition: this had to be one of his two boys. "Leo?" he said.

"No, papa. Look again."

Joel slapped his brush into a paint rag; it wobbled like the head of a fish.

"Isaac, you must have inherited your brother's face. I'm not

34

disappointed that it's you. You're my oldest. Half a century goes by, and you can still call me 'papa.'"

"Papa, don't exaggerate. I wasn't in this world fifty years ago."

Isaac squinted at his father's unnatural coloring, heightened reds around eyes, cheeks, and nose, and blue on the bumps of the skull. Joel was wearing rouge. He had a scarf on his throat, and a bottle-green painter's smock that would have identified him as a portraitist in any setting. It was Joel's uniform at The Iroquois.

"I was expecting you, Isaac. I'm not surprised. Have you come to murder your papa?"

The forks under Isaac's burly jaw twisted up into his mouth, leaving him with a stingy smile.

"Papa, search me. I'm clean. You can't smuggle guns into Paris."

"Isaac, you could smuggle anything. Don't think I'm ignorant of your career. I may be a piece of shit, but I follow my boys. Marilyn's the name of your daughter. She's an Irish beauty. She carries husbands on her back. Isaac, are you shocked how much I know? A boy from Seventh Avenue who used to work for me, he's in Paris once a year. An international buyer, with millions in his pocket, he sips wine and talks about my family. What's Leo doing?"

"Leo's in jail," Isaac spit through his teeth.

The rouge jumped under Joel's eyes. He retreated into his painter's smock, rising over the easel with his blued skull. He was scanning the elevators for American bait. "I'm neglecting my business, Isaac. I can see I'll have a poor afternoon." He mentioned an address on the rue Vieille-du-Temple. "It's in the Marais, on top of the Rivoli. Just ask for the Jews. You'll find it, Isaac. It will take you a while. You can murder me when you get there."

Isaac left The Iroquois so his father could begin to hustle. On the rue Hamelin he took out a gigantic map of Paris and searched for the proper grid. With his policeman's logic he timed his walk at two hours. Isaac cut east, above the bend in the river, and landed on the Place des Etats-Unis.

Two men in shiny brown coats hovered close to Isaac looking for pigeons to feed. Isaac watched the play of their hands. Their pursuit of birds seemed elaborate to him (Isaac couldn't locate a smear of pigeon shit in the Place des Etats-Unis). The shiny coats belonged to a dip artist and his squire. Isaac appraised this pickpocket team with a cool turn of his mind. They can't be from South America. The Guzmanns (a tribe of pickpockets out of Peru) would never wear shiny coats. These are locals from Algeria, or Sicily. Starving kids with the soft, beautiful fingers of a girl.

The team broke apart to encircle Isaac. The squire, a boy with a scarred nose, bumped Isaac into the dip. The boy heard a terrible scream. The dip's hand was caught inside Isaac's raincoat. Isaac crunched the girlish fingers with a squeeze of his fist. He brought the dip down to his knees.

He didn't forget the other boy. The squire was the vicious one, Isaac could tell. The squire had his blade, a pathetic kitchen knife without a handle. He meant to skewer Isaac with it. But he couldn't draw blood from the Chief. Isaac cracked the boy once, behind the ear, and the squire shot across the Place des Etats-Unis. The Chief was growing fond of Paris.

He made the Tuileries with over an hour to spare. He liked the measurements of a long, dead garden. The tramps who collected at the borders of the Tuileries had an independence Isaac could admire. Dressed in warm coats, none of them shuffled after him, or acknowledged his presence.

Isaac's exhilaration began to fade on the rue de Rivoli. A gorgeous line of mounted police, with plumes down their backs and silver pots on their heads, made him think of his father's uniform. Isaac scowled. His anger increased against Joel. My father's a clown, he muttered to himself. A clown in a snot-green shirt.

The rue de Rivoli became a region of shabby department stores, with windows that had the defiled look of a battlefield, and soon Isaac was in the Marais. Narrow streets with hump-backed buildings spilled over into each other's lap at crazy, undefined angles. Chimney pots cropped out over Isaac's head like warts on a monstrous finger. He passed kosher butcher shops, restaurants that sold *"Boercht Romain"* and *"Salami Hongrois,"* signs that spit competing slogans (*"Israël Vaincre!"* and *"Halte à l'Agression Arabe"*), and a synagogue strictly for North Africans. Joel, who cursed the rabbis of New York, had gone religious in his old age.

Isaac regretted his trip; he should have visited London instead, the London of Whitechapel, where Joel's father came from; he'd been a petty merchant, hustling bloomers on Princelet Street, and a "deacon" of the Spitelfield synagogue. Even then the Sidels didn't pray; they were in charge of the synagogue's economic affairs and its soup kitchen for indigent Jews. They were all charitable men.

Isaac discovered Joel's place on the rue Vieille-du-Temple.

There seemed to be no court in reach, no passageway for him to use. He stood by the house until an old woman emerged from an opening in the wall. Isaac went inside.

He groveled in the dark, searching for nonexistent bannisters with both his palms; he touched greasy wood and roughage on a low ceiling. He came out in the back somewhere, sliding against a tricky doorsill. He was in a court with ravaged blue ground and a nest of sinking trees. He clumped towards a set of stairs. His father lived on the top floor.

Joel's mistress was Vietnamese (Sophie had never bothered to divorce her wandering husband); a woman with delicate jaws and exquisite bones around her eyes, she worked as a chambermaid at The Iroquois. Joel called her Mauricette. She couldn't have been over thirty, but away from The Iroquois Joel was a much younger man. He abandoned his bottle-green smock and the trappings of a portraitist, and sat in an old velvet shirt that forced Isaac to contend with the handsomeness of his father. Joel wasn't a clown at home. The rouge had been wiped off.

"Isaac, who ripped your coat?"

"It's nothing, papa. I met two pickpockets in the street. They wanted to dance with me. I refused. They won't be so nimble for the next couple of weeks."

Joel shrugged at Isaac's delivery; he couldn't unravel detective stories. He summoned Isaac to the table. The fragrance of perfectly cooked rice caught Isaac by the nose. He softened to his father's circumstance. Joel didn't need more than one room. All his articles were here.

They ate fish with their hands, sucking between the bones. Isaac drank a silky wine that growled in his throat. Joel didn't plague him until the end of the meal.

"A super detective with his kid brother sitting in jail—Isaac, there has to be a moral in it. Did he rape the Police Commissioner's wife?"

"Papa, he isn't inside with criminals, I swear. It's only a civil complaint. I wouldn't let perverts near Leo. I have a brother who thinks it's chivalrous to be deaf, dumb, and blind. He's free with his own guts, that Leo. He scratches his ass with a leaky pen and signs his life away. Now he's a slave. His ex-wife owns the teeth in his mouth. Leo runs with his testicles stabbing the floor. He can't catch up on his alimony."

"Isaac, I could raise five hundred dollars. How much does he need?"

"Don't talk money, papa, please. Wouldn't I help that miserable prick? He won't take a nickel. He enjoys his misery."

Isaac walked down the stairs with bandied knees. The wine had put a blush on his neck. He groped against the walls giggling like an idiot boy who'd escaped from his father's house. Wavering in the moist blue earth of his father's court, he grew lenient with Joel. His mother had been crazy long before Joel left. She picked through garbage cans, collecting foul cardboard and ugly pieces of string, while Joel had his millions. Isaac loved her, and had a fondness for her piles of junk, and the Arabs she brought home, beggars, failed musicians, and unemployed cooks, after scavenging on Atlantic Avenue, but why should his father elect to stay with a woman who had permanent whiskers and rust on her fingers that couldn't wash off?

Isaac liked Mauricette. She was no mean stepmother to him, and no simple appendage to his father, no superficial wife. She mingled her spit and blood with Joel's in that one salty room.

Isaac returned to his hotel near the Place Vendôme. He tried to nap; the metallic click of the telephone tore through his drowsiness. He didn't need the help of overseas operators. He recognized Coen's nasal hello.

"Come home, Isaac. Your mother's been hurt."

4.

—————

HEADQUARTERS was invaded with shock troops. You couldn't miss them in the corridors, the locker rooms, and the johns. They collected near the marble pillars on the ground floor, sucking bitter lozenges, men in black leather coats, with dirty eyes. They barked at each other and spit at low-grade detectives and ordinary clerks, who called them "crows" and "undertakers" because of the vast amounts of black leather. The "crows" worked out of competing offices. They were rivals, members of elite squads that belonged to the Chief of Detectives, the First Deputy, and the Police Commissioner himself. The PC had spoken with uncommon bluntness: he wanted the scumbags that wounded Sophie Sidel.

Isaac shunned the leather boys. They scattered behind their pillars when they saw the Chief. Isaac had his own squad, boys without leather coats, blue-eyed detectives, marksmen who never sneered. He went to his office, across the hall from

"Cowboy" Rosenblatt, the Jewish Chief of Detectives. Isaac had been gone three days, but his great oak desk was cluttered with memorandums and personal notes, letters of condolence from all the Irish chiefs at Headquarters, from the Mayor's office, from Newgate, the FBI man, who played gin rummy with the First Dep, from Barney Rosenblatt and the PC, and an old-fashioned blue card in the fine scrawl of First Deputy O'Roarke. His phone had been ringing continuously for an hour. He held the earpiece over his cheek and growled his name. He wasn't in the mood for Mordecai.

"Isaac, I heard about your mother. The neighborhood is up in arms. We're forming patrols, Isaac. We'll repay slap for slap. How's Sophie?"

"She's still in a coma."

"Sophie's a tough girl. She'll pull through."

Isaac understood the habits of an old friend. Mordecai wouldn't have called him at the office to cluck words about Sophie. He was a delicate man, Mordecai. He had to be angling for someone else.

"Is it Honey?" the Chief said. "She hasn't fled the coop again, has she? I can't grab her this morning. But I can lend you Brodsky, or Coen."

Isaac heard a sound that could have been Mordecai sighing, or an electrical hiss. "Honey's at home . . . it's Philip. Can't you visit him? Isaac, he's in a terrible way."

"Jesus Christ, my mother's lying in Bellevue with tubes sticking out of her, and you pester me with Philip. Has his chess game been deteriorating? Philip doesn't move off his ass. So long, Mordecai."

Mordecai, Philip, and Isaac had been the three big brains of Seward Park High. Stalwarts of the chess club, devotees of

42

Sergei Eisenstein and Dashiell Hammett, they were insep-
arable in 1943, 1944, and 1945. But Mordecai and Philip remained visionaries, and Isaac joined the police. He screamed
for Pimloe, who ran the First Deputy's rat squad whenever
Isaac was away. Pimloe arrived with his clipboard and a gold-
nubbed fountain pen. He was wearing his Harvard Phi Beta
Kappa key. Isaac despised Pimloe's key. He'd had four miserable semesters at Columbia College, living in a monk's closet
on Morningside Heights.

"Where's Coen?"

"He's out tracking leads, like everybody else." Pimloe waved
the clipboard, which held a detailed map of lower Manhattan,
with green boxes for City parks, and a blue star for Headquarters; the map was littered with marks from Pimloe's
fountain pen. "Isaac, they hit twenty places last week. Six
between Essex and the Bowery, six in Chinatown, five in
Little Italy, one in SoHo, and two on Hudson Street. Barney
calls them the lollipop kids. Some old guinzo in Little Italy
swears they came into his store sucking lollipops."

"Herbert, are you cooperating with Barney Rosenblatt?"

"Isaac, you can't shove Cowboy out of this. The PC is
backing him up."

"I'll shove when I have to shove. Herbert, there's more than
one gang working the streets. Could be your map is a little
off, and we've got a whole bunch of lollipops on our hands."

"Isaac, it fits. They punch old people. They wear masks.
They won't take money."

"What's your theory, Herbert? Tell me your thoughts."

"Freaks. Definitely freaks. They attack, hide, and attack.
A fucking lollipop war."

"Is my mother included in your theory?"

"Isaac, what do you mean? That was strictly random. It could have been any old woman in a store."

"Random, my ass. Somebody's sending me a kite, and I can't figure why. Herbert, what have you got?"

Pimloe led the Chief to his favored niche outside the interrogation room on the second floor. They stared through the one-way mirror at the suspects Pimloe, Barney Rosenblatt, and the "crows" had rounded up for Isaac: retards from an Eighth Avenue hotel, winos fresh from Chinatown, a black whore with scabs on her knees, runaways from a New Jersey mental hospital, and two Puerto Rican cops disguised as pimps, so that Isaac could have a spectacular lineup. He scanned the faces only once, his lip curling high. "Let 'em go."

Isaac went around the corner to Margedonna's Bar and Grille. The barman wouldn't grin. Isaac tried the back room, where the Chief of Detectives was sitting with his "crows," their black leather coats humped against the wall on a line of pegs. Isaac approached Barney Rosenblatt's long table. None of the "crows" stood up for him. They stuffed their cheeks with eggplant and watched.

Barney Rosenblatt was the number-one Jew cop in the City of New York. He hated Isaac more than the Irish chiefs who surrounded him. Isaac undermined Barney's detectives with his squad of rats and personal spies. Both of them were officers in the Hands of Esau, a police fraternity for Jews. They squabbled here as much as they did at Headquarters. The Hands of Esau was in constant jeopardy on account of them.

Barney wore a Colt with his name and rank engraved right over the trigger, and a quick-draw holster with tassels at the bottom, like Buffalo Bill. Sliding out from the table, he gripped the holster's beard to prevent the Colt from stabbing him in the belly. The "crows" had swallowed too many red peppers: their eyes watered at the vision of Barney embracing Isaac. Were these burly men or dancing bears?

There was nothing sanctimonious about Cowboy's embrace. He squeezed Isaac's ribs with devotion. Barney wasn't a piddling warrior; he shared the grief of his enemies.

But Isaac hadn't interrupted Cowboy's lunch for a bearhug, and the smell of Chianti in a bottle brushed with straw. "Don't try to steal chickens off me, Barney. Stay out of my coop. I can handle this alone."

"Who's a chicken thief?" Cowboy said. He fought back his desire to take Isaac by the ears and throw him under the table.

"If there's a riddle, I'll solve it. The persons who touched my mother will have to deal with me."

"No vendettas, Isaac. This is police business. I can bring the whole Manhattan South down on those freaks, whoever they are."

"Barney, I don't want your boys rushing in and out. It's my caper. Hands off."

"Isaac, who have you got? Blue Eyes? That imbecile couldn't find his dick in the street."

"Barney, don't curse. You're talking about my man."

Cowboy had to let him go. As Chief of Detectives, he stood above the ladders that inspectors had to climb. But the First Deputy was dying of cancer, and the cop that inherited the First Dep's chair controlled the City police. Barney didn't have to guess who O'Roarke's heir would be. Still, he was in a celebrating mood. His oldest daughter, a spinster of thirty-two, would be a bride in eight days. This was Barney's last unmarried child. What had Isaac accomplished? He'd married off the same daughter three times.

Isaac didn't signal upstairs for Brodsky; a chauffeur could distract his mind. He rode in a cab, unwilling to discuss sugar scares, crime, or the weather.

The driver figured Isaac was a pornography czar, or a manager of small-time queens: no one had ever asked him to cruise the all-night movie houses on Forty-second Street. "That's the one," Isaac said, jumping out of the cab. The driver saw him disappear into the foyers of the Tivoli Theatre. He couldn't believe Isaac's gall. "The guy must think he's invisible. He walks through ticket windows."

Isaac foraged in the back rows. He couldn't borrow a flashlight from a Tivoli usher. Wadsworth, the man he wanted, would have hidden from him. He avoided the male prostitutes who were soliciting near the aisles. "Need a finger, baby? It'll cost you. Six dollars an inch." Isaac could have put them away, but he would have lost his man. He had to protect Wadsworth's house.

He heard a low crackle behind him. "*Vas machst du*, Isaac?" The Chief had to laugh. Wadsworth wouldn't recognize the fact that Isaac was an English-American Jew without a Yiddish vocabulary.

"Wadsworth, I'm doing fine."

Wadsworth was an albino, a milky nigger with pink eyes. He couldn't survive in sunlight. Wadsworth needed twenty-four hours of dark. He lived at the Tivoli, rinsing his mouth in the water fountain, doing his underwear in the sink, sneaking out after midnight, and returning to the theatre before the sun had a chance to rise. He existed on buttered popcorn and candy bars from the Tivoli's machines. He could sit through cartoons, features, and coming attractions in one position. Wadsworth claimed he never had to sleep.

"Did you look after my uncles, Isaac? My uncles are important to me."

"I'm trying, Wads. I can't jump over the civil service lists. But there may be room for a typist with the Department of Parks."

"Isaac, my uncles can't type."

The Chief had to groom Wadsworth with favors, little and big. He found temporary jobs for Wadsworth's long family of uncles, cousins, and friends. Wadsworth would take no profit for himself. He was the best informant Isaac ever had. A burglar by trade, and a sometime arsonist, he sold watches and shoes to firemen, sanitation workers, and the sons of mafiosi. Connected uptown and downtown with pickpockets, shylocks, and pinkie-breakers, Wadsworth cornered information before it hit the street.

"Isaac, if you're here about your mom, I can't help. Motherfuckers with masks, busting faces without putting a finger in the till, that sounds like amateur stuff."

"Or a hate job. Wadsworth, do you know anybody who dislikes me so much he'd send a gang of rotten kids to grab my tail?"

"Isaac, you asking me if you got enemies? I can name ten cops who'd love to murder you, including Cowboy Rosenblatt."

"I could name twenty, but this isn't the work of a cop. What about the Guzmanns?"

Gamblers and pickpockets from the Bronx, the Guzmanns were becoming a tribe of pimps. They had entered Isaac's borough to find chicken bait, thirteen-year-olds, all of them white, and Isaac vowed to drive the Guzmanns out of Manhattan. He stationed his men at the bus terminals to frustrate their ability to snatch young girls. "Wadsworth, are the Guzmanns paying me back?"

"Na," Wadsworth said, showing his pale lip. "The Guzmanns have feelings. They wouldn't hit on your mother. They'd come direct to you." The deep red of his pupils burned in the dusty air of the Tivoli; Isaac had to look away from Wadsworth's eyes. Wadsworth said, "Try Amerigo."

"Why would Amerigo come after me?"

"He's been grumbling, Isaac, that's all I know. He thinks you're sleeping with the FBI's."

"Wadsworth, that's office politics. The First Dep has to be polite. We use their labs sometimes. But Newgate's a dummy. Why would I sleep with him?"

"Don't explain it to me, man. Save it for Amerigo."

Isaac blinked in the raw sunlight outside the Tivoli. He was a cop who wasn't used to caves. He scowled at Inspector Pimloe's theories on the lollipop gang. His office had come up with shit, stupid shit. Pimloe brought Isaac a gallery of hobos and talked of random attacks. Isaac had other ideas about these lollipops. They scared Ida, his fiancée, raided his hangout on Essex Street, and beat up his mother in a single night. They wanted Isaac to get the news. Could Amerigo Genussa be their benefactor, the man who fingered Isaac, and supplied the kids with masks and all-day suckers?

Amerigo was president of the Garibaldi social club and the *padrone* of Mulberry Street. Before he went into real estate and bought up a sixth of Little Italy, he'd been a miraculous chef. He had to give up the Caffè da Amerigo to supervise his holdings and safeguard the streets. The Puerto Ricans were making inroads, Chinamen were grabbing vacant buildings north of Canal, but Amerigo had kept out the blacks. His hirelings liked to boast that their mammas and girlfriends couldn't see a black face a half mile around the Garibaldi social club, unless it belonged to a cop, or an FBI man.

The Garibaldis were having a personal war with the FBI, whose scarecrows and paid informers swarmed Amerigo's streets, tapped his telephones, peeked in his window, dug wires into his walls, tried to flirt with the daughters of Mulberry grocers, bakers, and ravioli men.

Isaac took a second cab down to Grand Street. He visited the fruit stand of Murray Baldassare, across from Ferrara's pastry house. Murray had been a marginal stoolpigeon, registered with the First Deputy's office, until Isaac turned him over to Newgate. Now he was Newgate's decoy, a fink for the FBI. Newgate financed Murray's career as a fruitman, throwing four thousand dollars into the stand. Murray had no time for the fruit. Women from the neighborhood were fleecing him out of his bundles of tangerines. Murray was supposed to spy on Ferrara's; Newgate had the notion that the *dons* of Grand Street conducted their business over Ferrara's coffee mugs and trays of Sicilian pastry. There wasn't a child in Little Italy over the age of six who didn't know that Murray Baldassare was a fink. He stayed alive because he had nothing to feed Newgate. Amerigo himself ate Murray's tangerines.

Murray recoiled at the image of Isaac shining through the tiny window of his stand. He developed hiccups that knocked underneath his lungs. Isaac had to drive a fist into Murray's shoulder before the fruitman could get back his speech. The tangerines had a scarlet flush; their skins bled for Isaac. He swiped one from Murray's window, its skin tearing under the force of Isaac's yellow nail. The nectar inside was frozen to the strings that covered the fruit.

"Chief," Murray said, "why come here? You want to see me dead?"

Isaac licked his fingers. "Relax, Murray. Amerigo knows you were married to me. He won't hurt you."

"It aint Amerigo. It's the FBI's. Newgate'll cripple me. You think he's stupid? He can figure for himself. The reports I'm shoving him are a bunch of crap. He'll say me, you, and Amerigo are dancing on his head."

"Didn't I put you in business, Murray? Don't complain. You're a celebrity now. Nobody ever copped a fruit stand off the FBI's before."

"Isaac, I'm begging you, get me out of this."

Isaac put the injured tangerine back in Murray's window.

"Talk to me, Murray. You watch the street. Has Amerigo been hiring any goons lately?"

Murray's eyes wandered from the ceiling to Isaac's shoes. "I think so."

"How many, Murray, how many has he hired?"

"Three or four."

"Are they lollipops—kids? One of them a young girl? Did he send them to stomp on my mother?"

Quivers rose inside Murray's cheeks that went beyond the possibility of a bluff. "Your mother, Isaac? . . . Newgate never told me. Who could do such a terrible thing?"

Isaac made the corner, with Murray caught behind his glass, tangerines up to his groin, his trunk twisted and inert, and his face turned mechanical: dim leering eyes in a nest of hollows. He was a discard, a spy that Isaac had manufactured, stroked, groomed, and shelved, and then fobbed off on the FBI.

The Chief was remorseful about Murray. But Newgate had hounded the First Dep for one of Isaac's famous spies, and Murray was the spy Isaac could spare. He passed the social clubs of Mulberry Street, their windows shuttered with broad stripes of green paint, with the inevitable "MEMBERS ONLY" scratched into the green.

Isaac entered the Garibaldi club. The members glared at him, but no one threw him out. The Garibaldis endured his policeman's smell, his blunt tie, his calfskin shoes, his orange socks, and the desecration of a pistol in their rooms. Most of them were men over sixty, snug in the thermal underwear exposed at their ankles and their wrists. They were drinking black coffee mixed with anisette, or cappuccinos from the Garibaldi's big machine.

Growls escaped from Isaac's stomach. He was addicted to coffee with steamed milk. He shunned the espresso joints of Bleecker and MacDougal, the Caffè Borgia, where they drowned your coffee in whipped cream, the Verdi, with its bits of chocolate in the foam, and the Reggio, which had a tolerable caffè moka, but little else. Isaac went to Vinnie's luncheonette on Sullivan, where he could enjoy his cappuccinos in a simple glass, or Manganaro's on Ninth Avenue, if he was in the mood to banter with the countermen, who begrudged pulling the handles of their espresso machine.

The aroma of coffee inside the Garibaldi club, thickened by the push of radiators, could drive a cop mad. The Garibaldis had the best cappuccinos in New York. You couldn't attribute this to the wonders of a machine that produced sensational foam and squeezed boiling water through a bed of coffee grounds. It was the devotion of the Garibaldis themselves, who wouldn't consider making cappuccinos for hire.

Amerigo Genussa sat among the Garibaldis in a stunning red shirt that was wide in the sleeves. A man no older than Isaac, with scars around the eyes from fights he'd had in the kitchens of Little Italy, he was concentrating on his game of dominoes.

Isaac resolved not to break the silence at the Garibaldi club. He would outlast dominoes, cappuccino mugs, Amerigo's hatred for him. But the whistling heat off the radiators clung to Isaac, attacking the skin behind his ears. The redness of Amerigo's shirt turned bitter in Isaac's mouth, and he could taste the dry surface of the dominoes. "You want a coffee, Isaac?"

"No."

Amerigo brought two mugs down from the shelves. Slyly, without a crease in his nostrils, Isaac watched the coffee-making. The machine shivered with a sucking noise as Amerigo steamed the milk. He cranked the lever, and coffee poured from two metal fangs.

"It hurts me to have a sullen man in my club. Stay out if you can't smile."

He pushed one of the mugs at Isaac. The Chief stared at the bubbles in the milk. "Bite my fist, landlord, but don't you ever go near my mother again. I'll kill you so slow, your brains will leak into your ear before you have the chance to die."

"Isaac, I fuck you where you breathe. If I wanted your mother, I wouldn't have messed up the job."

The Garibaldis fingered their dominoes while Isaac and Amerigo grimaced at one another near the cappuccino mugs.

"Tell me you haven't been hiring goons off the street."

"Sure I'm hiring. You think your mother was the only casualty? The little bastards come into my precincts, slap Mrs. Pasquino over the head, demolish her bakery, and run home to Jewtown so they can eat their kosher baloney. Isaac, I'll break their feet."

"Amerigo, are you saying it's a gang of rabbinical students? A Jewish karate club? Take a walk for yourself."

"Two of them are Yids, definitely. A boy and a girl. The last one's some kind of nigger. If he's not a spade, then he's a Turk or a Jap. Isaac, it's gotta be."

Isaac dug his jaw into the cappuccino mug. He licked the coffee, his throat purring at the taste of browned milk. "Amerigo, I'll handle these lollipops. Call off your goons."

"Impossible. Isaac, why argue? We're both soldiers. You have your precincts, I have mine. How's your daughter? Did she make a good marriage this time?"

"She's okay," Isaac said, with coffee in his teeth. "She has an architect." Could he tell the landlord that Marilyn was running wild? That she was on the loose with lollipops stalking the streets?

"And your brother Leo, is he out of his troubles yet?"

"Leo's doing fine."

The coffee oozed through Isaac's system, causing the skin on his knees to curl, and whishing into the pockets around his eyes. Isaac would have sold his daughter for a second cappuccino. The Garibaldis had him in their grip.

"Isaac, I hear your boyfriend has his own pillow at Headquarters. Now he doesn't have to snore in the Commissioner's lap."

"Landlord, I can't count all my boyfriends. Identify him for me."

53

"Newgate."

"Jesus," Isaac said, coming out of his coffee lull. "How can Newgate hurt you? He'd drown in the puddles if the PC didn't hold his hand."

"Isaac, he gives me a bad name. He frightens young Italian mothers with his ugly eyes. The mothers say Newgate's a witch. They could have deformed babies, and I'll get the blame. What's he got against the Italian race? Does he think Sicily was the devil's country? Half my buildings have busted toilets. I'm swimming in shit with my plumber's boots, and that schmuck talks about organized crime?"

"Complain to Cowboy, not me. Cowboy's the one who loves the FBI's." Isaac sucked at the bottom of the mug with the spaces between his teeth. "Amerigo, keep your goons on your side of the Bowery. If I catch them near Essex Street, they won't be in any condition to search for lollipops."

He got up without fantasies of destruction in his head. He wouldn't spit on dominoes, smash the espresso machine, bring the Garibaldis to Headquarters. He had no grudge against Amerigo Genussa. He walked around the tables and landed in the street.

5.

Marilyn didn't mourn her penniless state. Shuffling from Bellevue to Coen's to the Crosby Street jail, she narrowed her problems down to the question of logistics: how could she avoid her father on her father's turf? She sat in Bellevue with her Jewish grandmother, surrounded by bottles and tubes that could draw the wastes out of Sophie and drip vital sugars into her body. Sophie's bruises had turned yellowish. The coma she was in wasn't absolute. She would come out of her sleep to frown at the pipes in her nose and signal to Marilyn with her dry tongue. Marilyn couldn't gauge the extent of Sophie's recognition. Was Sophie calling for a nurse or mouthing "Kathleen," the name of Marilyn's mother?

"I'm with you, grandma Sophie. Kathleen's daughter. Your grandchild Marilyn."

She escaped the stare of interns and orderlies on the prowl. Isaac could be behind the door. He had a whole catalogue of spies to trap her with; men in hospital coats, detectives wearing powder and a false moustache, who would point a finger at Isaac's skinny daughter and cluck for the Chief. She saw this type of man scrounging on Crosby Street. She was carrying cookies for uncle Leo that she made with flour from Coen's single pantry shelf. The man had pieces of charcoal around his lips. He tried to mimic the auras of a bum. He blew on his knuckles, tore at the threads of his coat, bit hairs off his wrinkled scarf. Marilyn laughed at the flaws in his disguise. The cop had protected feet: only a police bum would walk around in Florsheim shoes.

A crease near the eyes disturbed Marilyn. "Brian Connell," she said without embarrassment. She knew him from Echo Park, and her junior-high-school days. She'd had several "sweethearts." Brian was one of them.

"Mary?" he said. He couldn't understand how a girlie could pinpoint him under a coat, a hairy scarf, and a blackened face.

"I'm Marilyn. Marilyn Sidel."

The cop blew on his knuckles again. He had gorgeous teeth. Memories of Marilyn ruined his charcoal complexion. His cheeks burned with color as he recollected a bony girl with big tits.

"Marilyn, it's insane I should meet you at the bottom of Manhattan. I'm with the anti-crime boys. I work out of Elizabeth Street. The bosses are sitting on our heads. They'll murder us if we can't produce the mutts that hit your grandmother. That's why I'm in my Bowery clothes."

Marilyn felt silly shaking the paw of an old, old boyfriend, someone who'd licked her flesh eleven years ago. Brian had never been shy with her; now he rocked on his Florsheims, knuckles in his mouth. He's afraid of my father, Marilyn guessed. She showed him the cookies. "I have to deliver them to my uncle. See you around, Brian. Goodbye."

Brian moved his jaw in a cunning way. He wouldn't release Marilyn's hand. He had to bend one knee to hide his erection from her.

"Marilyn, don't be brief. We could divide Marble Hill and the North Bronx between ourselves. We share the same freaky past. Have a beer with me."

Brian contemplated a quick romance. If he could get close to Marilyn, blow on her nipples until she was crazy about him, he would have an opening to Isaac. Brian needed a big Jew. (None of the Irish rabbis at Headquarters had picked him up.) Isaac was the First Deputy's whip and high chief of all the rabbis, white, black, and Puerto Rican. Brian couldn't fail once he had Isaac for a "father-in-law." So he escorted Marilyn to a bar on Spring Street, fondling his visions of a detective's shield.

The barkeep winked at Marilyn, and stuck a bottle of gin in Brian's arm. Cradling the bottle, Brian waltzed around the bar stools in his floppy coat. He had to gesture three times with his long neck before Marilyn would follow him into the back room. "I thought we were drinking beer," she said. The door clicked shut behind her.

"Brian, this is a real Bronx reunion. You haven't changed any of your tricks."

"It's damp at the bar. In here we can have some quiet." Brian was in a quandary: should he make her first, or squeeze promises out of her to whisper his name and badge number in Isaac's ear? "Marilyn, tell me about your family."

57

"What's there to tell? I'm a victim of combat fatigue. I've been through three husbands. Brian, how many wives do you have?"

Mother of Mercy, she's still a fucking tramp, Brian sang to himself. He made no attempt now to hide his erection.

"I'm single, Marilyn, I swear. Which husband did you like best?"

Marilyn had to lie. "I can't remember." She wouldn't tell him about the husband she adored, her first one, Larry, a blond boy with a lisp, whom she brutalized with her affectionate rages and jealousies. Reared by Kathleen, the real estate goddess, and Isaac the Pure, she'd been much too tough for a blond boy. The beautiful Larry ran away. Coen, the blue-eyed orphan, could remind her of him.

Brian sucked on his bottle with an angel's smile. He was thinking of gangbangs in cellars, weightlifting rooms, and the woods of Isham Park, with Marilyn satisfying each and every star of the Inwood Hill Athletic Club, her lean body trembling under the impact of Brian and his friends, who could assuage their dread of purgatory with the knowledge that Marilyn wasn't wholly Irish. The boys interpreted her willingness to undress as a spiteful Jewish streak.

Brian rinsed his tongue in sweet alcohol. His smile turned sullen, giving his teeth a wolfish edge. Marilyn's three husbands enraged him. Whore, bitch, he babbled in his head, she's always going down for bunches of three. He poked a finger into Marilyn's blouse. The finger stood on her collarbone. Brian didn't know where to explore. His brains were swollen with gin.

Marilyn removed the finger from her chest without cursing Brian. She wasn't mean. She had cookies to deliver. She saw

Brian's cheeks explode. The gin was in her face. The blouse came off her shoulders in one hard rip. Brian's knuckles mashed against her cheekbone. She had little mousies under her eye. She wanted to vomit blood. Brian stooped with his thumbs in her hips, and Marilyn's skirt fell under her knees. The cloth around her ankles prevented her from kicking him. She made feeble shoves with her elbows. Brian knocked her to the floor.

He was struggling with Marilyn of Isham Park. He could eclipse husbands, wedding bands, and marriage beds with the mesh pants he took from her and rubbed in his fist. She was Brian's whore child. Isaac didn't exist. The split of her bosoms, the trembling line of her ribs, the rise and fall of her complicated navel, proved to him she was a creature of the cellars, someone with tainted blood and a vague history. He pushed her knees apart and dug with his hand. He tolerated scratching elbows and the mischief of a whore's fingernails. He kept his knuckles in Marilyn's eye. He snapped her head back with a tug of her scalp. He punched her until she grew quiet.

Marilyn tried to think of Larry. But she started to cry. So she thought of Coen. She imagined the shape of his neck, the aroma of talcum powder on Amsterdam Avenue, the feel of Coen's blond knee, and the pressure that knifed down from her bosoms to her shanks eased a bit. Brian figured she had to be crazy when he heard her mumble "Blue Eyes."

His partners caught him reciting Hail Marys behind a pile of beards. They dragged him out of the property closet, glowering at the scratches on his face. These were the anti-crime boys, and they couldn't afford to have their reputation besmirched by a religious freak. The house bulls would laugh at them. Their own sergeant would pass them off as imbeciles. They were sworn to find the lollipop gang, to impress Headquarters with their ability to work undercover and wear a sensational disguise. "Brian, wake up."

He clasped his partners' knees and cried into their trouser cuffs. "Isaac is gonna kill me."

"Brian, what would big Isaac want with you?"

"I fucked his daughter," Brian said.

They smiled and looked at Brian with new respect.

"She's a bimbo who collects wedding rings. I had to beat her up."

His partners were horrified. They shook Brian off their cuffs. Big Isaac could reach into any precinct and squash a cop in bum's clothes. But if Isaac found Brian Connell, he might sink all of them. "Get back into the closet," they said.

Brian crawled on his belly like a snake in a wool stocking. Loose hair from a moustache on the shelf drifted down to him, and Brian had to sneeze. It was nasty in the dark. He promised the Holy Mother two consecutive novenas if She would make Isaac disappear. The closet opened. He could see into his partners' mouths. "It's only Blue Eyes," they said.

They hauled him out again, tickling him under his holster. Brian guffawed. "Isaac's afraid of us. He sends his rat to meet with me. I'll bury Coen. Just watch."

Coen had baffled the anti-crime boys. He came to their precinct with stubble on his chin. They remembered him in herringbone; Isaac loved to groom the First Deputy's spies. His squad of manicured detectives had become a legend in Manhattan stationhouses, where a cop learned to distrust any sweet-looking boy without a little dirt under his nails. But Coen was in a lumber jacket and pants that were as grubby as Brian's. The anti-crime boys hunched near the walls so that Coen could have a direct path to Brian in their locker room.

"Brian Connell?" he said in his natural voice.

Brian didn't like being greeted by a nasal man. He knew he had quicker hands than Blue Eyes. He stuck his service revolver in Coen's jaw. "You think you can shame me in front of my own squad? Who told you to speak my name? You'd better ask permission, Mr. Blue Eyes."

Coen didn't blink with a Police Special in his jaw. The gun's nose was grinding into his back teeth. The boys near the wall whispered something about coroners and morgues for Coen. Brian couldn't get Coen to grimace. The corners of his mouth wouldn't turn. The disintegrating flecks of color in his irises had little to do with Brian. Coen's eyes whirled independent of the locker room. Brian put the gun away. He sensed the futility of his bluff. Blue Eyes was merciless.

Brian sank into the property closet door, his knees dropping out from under him. He couldn't breathe until he was below the level of Coen's eyes. Stirring air through his pockets, he considered Isaac's mysterious ways. The Chief wouldn't enter a locker room. He'd hire Coen to do his killings. Brian was remorseful now that he bungled his drinking party with Marilyn. He could have been one of Isaac's deadly angels.

He was afraid to touch Coen, to embrace a killer's knee. So he sobbed with his thumbs in his sleeves. "Manfred, never mind what Isaac says. Me and Marilyn once were going steady. Check it out. I didn't swipe her off the street . . . Manfred, she knew me from Echo Park. We had accordion lessons together at the parish . . . some girl. She was the first Jewish mick I ever saw."

How could Coen pull the ears of a man this close to the ground? Marilyn had wandered into his apartment an hour ago, naked under her coat, her cheeks puffed out, and blood in her nose. Coen realized these markings couldn't be accidental. Her head was mapped too methodically with swollen ruins. He discovered her skirt, blouse, and shredded pants among the cookies in her shopping bag. He couldn't believe this was Isaac's work. If the Chief had been in the mood for corporal punishment, he wouldn't have broken Marilyn's face. He would have gone to Manfred, who was hiding her from him. Coen took advantage of Marilyn's dizziness. He was able to shake Brian Connell's name out of her. He rushed down to Elizabeth Street. Coen didn't have Isaac's agility. He was poor at contriving schemes. He meant to slap Brian, and then what? Should he undress Brian in the stationhouse, have him crawl without his clothes?

Brian's sobs made Coen miserable. The cop's ears were wet. Coen distrusted the anti-crime boys. They were meddlers who liked to play detective in the street. He lost his desire to steal Brian's pants.

"Listen to me, you glom. Wherever Marilyn goes, you walk the opposite way. If you're ever in her neighborhood, you'll wish Manhattan didn't exist."

Brian's partners remained near the walls with their guts sucked in. They didn't have the clout of a blue-eyed detective. They were only glorified patrolmen, cops out of uniform, so they couldn't pounce on Coen. Isaac would have flopped the entire squad, fed them to niggers and man-eating sharks in the Bronx.

From Elizabeth Street Coen went on a tour of youth centers in the lower East Side. He was scouting for ferocious teenagers, boys and girls who might be lollipops. His third stop was a Jewish center at Rivington and Suffolk. He noticed a remarkable absence of skullcaps and religious memorabilia. Where were the Jews of Suffolk Street?

The center proliferated with Chinese boys, Latinos, blacks, and surly whites from Seward Park. Its oblong game room looked as if it had to confront a nightly whirlwind. The walls were plundered dry, the woodwork having disappeared, and holes existing where ornaments and basketball fixtures should have been.

There was a series of huge, snaking genitals on the front wall, signed by "Esther Rose." The artist had been meticulous about pubic hair, stippling it in with eye shadow and different shades of lipstick. "Esther Rose" seemed to have a slanted mind; her clitorises were much taller than her cocks. Coen enjoyed the lipstick art. "Esther Rose" had put little eyeballs and chicletlike teeth around the swads of pubic hair.

Slogans were scrawled in shocking pink under "Esther Rose's" genitals.

"RUPERT SAYS WE'LL ALL DISAPPEAR IF ARABS AND JEWS DON'T KISS"

"THE GROSS NATIONAL PRODUCT IS THE INVENTION OF BANKERS WITH A LOW SEMEN COUNT"

"RUPERT SAYS GEORGE WASHINGTON WILL BE FORGOTTEN LONG BEFORE WILLIE MAYS"

"SACHS AND GIMBEL'S ARE THE WHORES OF NEW YORK, RUPERT SAYS"

Coen couldn't devote himself to Rupert's sayings. He had to mingle with the center's population, cast about for suspicious objects and faces, fish for a gang of womanbeaters.

Boys in jerseys and brimless hats milled from corner to corner, avoiding Coen and his lumber jacket. Their vocabulary baffled him until he realized that "red mountain," "torro," and "colony" were the names of cheap wines.

The baby winos began to sneer at Coen. They collected around a ping-pong table that consisted of a crooked green net and a series of hills. The local champion, a loud, argumentative boy with wiry hair, challenged the winos to a game if they could come up with fifty cents. The winos were too poor. So the champion enticed Coen with his eyebrows and a suck of his lips. "Hey bro', got some pocket money?" Coen agreed to play.

The winos hooted at him. They smelled another victim of the hilly ping-pong table. Coen acknowledged their noises with a grin. They were reasonable hoodlums. He was hoping to flush them out, find the lollipops through them. The champion had a sponge bat with fresh sheets of rubber glued on. He gave Coen a sandpaper bat worn down to the wood. Coen didn't worry. Ping-pong was his game. He'd perfected his strokes at an uptown club after his wife divorced him.

The champion had an illegal serve. He wouldn't throw up the ball. He held it in his fingers, and slapped at it while turning his wrist. The ball sped across the table with an evil spin. The champion had memorized the peculiar surfaces of this table; he know every hill, every dull spot, every dip in the net. But Coen wasn't a country player. He minimized the boy's advantages by blocking the ball with his shallow bat. He added a delicate push, and the ball went back over the net with the same exact spin. The champion stared at the ball. No one had ever made him hit his own spins. He grew demoralized after three short volleys with Coen. He began eating the rubber off his bat.

The winos refused to cheer. They rolled their eyes with a menace Coen couldn't ignore. He'd never seen fourteen-year-olds with such dispassionate faces: they had the glint of hard, old men. They marched around Coen, berating him in a babble of Spanish and English.

"Who is this *borinqueña?*"

"*Yo no sé,* man, but I think he came down to fuck with us. Bring Stanley."

"Stanley'll picadillo him for hustling fifty cents."

Stanley was a Chinese boy with spectacular biceps. He arrived in a Bruce Lee sweatshirt with ripped-off sleeves. Coen wouldn't pay court to the boy's muscular twitch. Biceps couldn't frighten him. Stanley had a beautiful face. That's what disturbed Coen. Muscles seemed incongruous with soft eyes. The winos' monkeyish glint and bitter cheeks were missing from the boy.

He had a perfectly tolerant voice. "Mister, what do you want from us?"

"A little news," Coen said.

The baby winos squeezed their eyebrows together. They were appraising Coen. A shrimp like him couldn't take them by surprise. They had a gift for smelling cops. Cops don't play ping-pong, they decided among themselves.

"Hey sister, you from the Board of Ed? You know what we do to truant officers? We suck their noses and tickle them to death."

"You gotta be wrong, bro' . . . this *muchacha* is a Treasury man. He saw you licking on a bottle, and he's trying to collect his whiskey tax."

"You full of shit. I say he's an uptown fairy. He's here to redecorate."

Coen unbuttoned his lumber jacket. He was going to scratch himself. But the spring in his holster had loosened during the ping-pong game, and his gun fell out. The winos fluttered near the gun. "*Mira, mira,* look what uncle brought. Spread out, man." Coen was chagrined; he hadn't intended to menace the winos with a gun. They ran from him. The Chinese boy was the only one who stayed.

"I'll ask him about the lollipop gang," Coen mouthed to himself, trusting Stanley's intelligence. The center cleared out, leaving Coen an uncomplicated view of rotting walls and broken electrical wire. Stanley wouldn't move. Coen was about to mention the lollipops when he felt two enormous claws climb on his chest and throw him over the ping-pong table. He could have sworn Stanley's ankles never left the ground. The boy had kicked air without going into a crouch or tightening his beautiful face, and he crashed into Coen's lungs with his feet. Coen was on the floor with a pain scooping under his heart that rattled his throat and brought his guts into his mouth. He figured he would have to die. But his lungs were blowing in and out. Blood rushed into his head. Coen stood up. He was thinking lollipops again.

6.

THE owners of the Ludlow Street restaurant were angry at Ida Stutz. They could no longer work her twelve hours a day. Ida had grown sullen. She was insisting on her rights to a genuine lunch break. The Chief hadn't knocked on the restaurant's cloudy window since he returned to America, and Ida meant to find him.

She was worried about Isaac. He'd become a skinny inspector if she couldn't fill him with mushrooms and barley soup. It wasn't in her nature to be stingy with men. Isaac needed her flesh to rid himself of anxieties and the strain of being a father, husband, son, and brainy cop. Ida simplified his life. She knew he had a missing daughter, a shrill wife, and a mother in the hospital, poor Sophie, who took Arabs into her bed. Ida was on her way to Rivington Street, and Isaac's rooms. She would freshen the earth in his flower pots, scrub the inside of his refrigerator, wait for him by the fire escape.

The streets had a pernicious look to Ida. The remains of boxes from the pickle factories flew across the gutters, bumping like fingers and limbs off a doll's body. The February wind could eat into wood, slice through the corners of the low, gutted buildings, make the old Jewish beggar on Broome Street sink his head into the middle of his overcoat, blow under the deepest layer of Ida's skirts, and pinch the seams of her powerful bloomers. Ida was praying for snow. The dark *snegu* of her Russian grandmother (the snow that fell near Delancey Street was more blue than white) could cake all the gutters with rich ice, hide the debris, force the pickle factories to conduct their business away from the sidewalks.

Ida didn't bemoan the past. It was no matter to her that the Essex Street market sold wigs instead of farmer cheese. The Cubans had come to Essex Street along with an influx of Israeli grocers. Ida welcomed them. She battled with the Israelis over her heathen principles, her distrust of promised lands and Jews with tanks, but she battled out of love. And the Cubans adored Ida's blintzes, although they couldn't pronounce the word.

Hands, rude hands, without mittens or gloves, snatched at her near Isaac's building, pulling her into a hallway. She was surrounded by a confusion of masks. She shivered at the hot, breathing eyes on top of her. Ida recognized the lollipop gang. This was the threesome that had visited her in the restaurant, stealing blintzes, fondling her breasts, and had gone around the corner to break Sophie's head. Ida could smell a girl's hair under one of the masks. Growls came out of the girl. The other two were quieter.

"Isaac's pussy," the girl said, holding Ida by the jaw. The two boys had to restrain her. "She's harmless," the shorter boy said. "Take a look."

The girl couldn't be placated so easily. "She goes down for him. It must rub off. A homely bitch is what I say." And the girl got up on her toes to grab hunks of Ida's hair. "Tell sweet Isaac regards from Esther Rose."

"Shut up," the shorter boy said.

The taller boy slouched against a row of bruised mailboxes, his body turning away from all the banter. As Ida pushed at the fingers tearing into her scalp, she felt the boy's restless moves. He was retreating from his friends. The shorter boy, wedged close to Ida and Esther Rose, brought Ida out of Esther's reach. "Get smart," he said. "That man's too piggy for you. He has shit in his ears. He made his name sucking off New York. Now the city's taking revenge."

"Let's fuck her," Esther rasped. "Let's fuck her under her fat clothes . . . it'll be like throwing harpoons in a whale. I'll bet she's filled with mush."

She whacked at Ida with the blade of her hand. The taller boy stumbled along the wall, catching metal pieces off the mailboxes with a shoulder. Esther nudged the other boy. "Are you with me, Rupe?"

He blunted Esther's chops with an elbow. "We're going . . . come on."

They pushed Ida deeper into the hall, packing her into the space behind a door, and ran, their masks struggling towards the street in a steady wave. Ida didn't whimper. It wasn't strictly fear that kept her behind the door. She couldn't figure out the three masks. What did they want with Isaac and her? She wished she could drown herself in the smoky air of the restaurant. Ida loved to breathe salmon and baked cottage cheese. She wallowed in her shoes, trying to hurl the wind out of her ankles. It was freezing in the hall.

Isaac was scratching his brain for logical enemies. He'd come to Bummy's chop house on East Broadway to interview Milton Gulavitch, a dispossessed murderer and thief with blood clots in both legs and a grudge against Isaac. Twenty years ago Gulavitch had been the "controller" of Brownsville and East New York. No dry cleaner in that long, muggy corridor between Brooklyn and Queens could survive without a license from Milton, who remained powerful in middle age because he had a legitimate means of protecting his empire: two of his brothers were homicide detectives in lower Manhattan. These younger Gulavitches, Myron and Jay, had their own slender business behind Little Italy; they fleeced Puerto Rican, Chinese, and Jewish grocers, and bloodied noses for the landlords and bondsmen of Baxter Street. Isaac, the boy detective, stumbled upon Myron and Jay, and helped send them into retirement and disgrace. Milton grieved for his brothers. He swore to take out Isaac's eyes; blind detectives couldn't squirrel into other men's affairs. He crossed the Williamsburg Bridge and waited for Isaac in Mendel's of Clinton Street, a bar inhabited by Jewish cops and hoods.

Isaac couldn't permit Gulavitch to scare him out of Mendel's bar. He was chubbier then, a boy with skin hanging off his fists. He arrived in a tweed suit, aware of the strength in Milton's thumbs, that ability to pluck eyeballs. Isaac put his blackjack and gun on Mendel's counter. He didn't want customers to think he was here on official business. Gulavitch laughed. He had nothing but thumbs in his pockets. With a deceptive, languid motion, he came off one hip to grab Isaac around the head. Isaac burrowed his eyes into the "controller's" chest, so Gulavitch had nowhere to dig. He hadn't anticipated such tactics from a boy; he left his face exposed. Isaac reached with a chubby hand. Knuckling hard, he split Gulavitch's eyebone. Gulavitch clutched his face. The customers around him opened their mouths in wonder and disgust. Gulavitch became Gula One Eye. He drifted out of circulation, his empire passing into other hands, and reappeared as Bummy Gilman's dishwasher and sweep after a lapse of fifteen years.

Isaac had contempt for Bummy, who fawned over Barney Rosenblatt and Jewish precinct captains, but he didn't come to wreck Bummy's place. "Where's Gula?" he said.

Bummy was nervous with Isaac in his bar. He couldn't get around the Chief, bribe him with lamb chops and pornographic shows. "Don't touch him, Isaac. He's senile."

"Good. But maybe he has a few grandchildren who run errands for him. I have to know."

"Isaac, he can't remember his name. If you blow on him, he'll fall down."

"Don't worry. I'll catch him before he falls."

Isaac went into Bummy's kitchen. It stank of animal fat and old men's sour pants. Milton Gulavitch was screwing warts out of a potato with his thumb. He held Isaac's attention with the furrows in a thumbnail. "Gula?"

Isaac wasn't paranoid about the old man. Gulavitch often

stood outside Headquarters to curse Isaac and cry for his brothers. Lately he'd been threatening to reassemble his empire and smack it over Isaac's head. Barney Rosenblatt offered to drag Gulavitch away. Isaac wouldn't allow it.

"Gula, listen. Do you have nephews and a niece in Brooklyn? Did you encourage them to hate me?"

Gulavitch looked up from the potato. "Die, Isaac. That's what you can do for me."

He wasn't wearing his patch, and Isaac had to stare into a blue socket, his own grizzly work. Spittle began to flow under Gulavitch's tongue. "Isaac, your prick will drop off one day, and then you'll be at my mercy."

Isaac closed the interview. He ignored Bummy's frowns at the bar and walked to Crosby Street. Dissatisfied, without a solution behind his big ears, he was going to see his brother. He could have gotten Leo past any guard or deputy warden, but Leo wouldn't budge. Isaac didn't have to growl Leo's name. The guards brought him into the reception room, shuddering under the eyes of the Chief. Leo was an embarrassment to them; each day he wore a prison shirt, the guards had to scrape their noses on Isaac's shit list. They were very jittery men.

"Leo, are they treating you with respect?" Isaac muttered, while the guards fled the room.

This scattering of the guards made Leo glum. He didn't want to be alone with his brother. "Isaac, you shouldn't have done that. They're good to me."

"Schmuck, they'd slap your brains if you weren't my brother. So how good can they be?"

"I don't care. It's a fact of nature. I'm invulnerable because of you." Leo shivered like a scarecrow in his loose shirt; he wasn't even safe inside a goddamned jail. Isaac could reach into every hole. Manhattan was his honey jar.

"Leo, I saw our dad. He's alive . . . doing portraits. He asked about you."

A sound broke out of Leo that was almost a snarl. "I have no dad."

Isaac was amazed by Leo's churning jaw. "I say he's alive. . . . Joel, Joel. I met him twice."

Leo clutched the little pocket on Isaac's vest. "There are no fucking Joels. Isaac, I'm warning you. Don't get me mad."

The pocket ripped. Isaac left his brother's fingers inside the torn seams. The violence to Isaac's pocket seemed to quiet Leo. He took his fingers away so he could cry into his knuckles. "Sophie's in the hospital on account of him. She'd be a saner person if that miserable furrier hadn't disappeared. You think she would have fallen in love with a junk shop? Isaac, you had your handgrips and your chess diagrams and your great chums, Philip and Mordecai. You didn't need a thing. What about me? Brother, I was slow. I couldn't hold a line of pawns, or make improvements in the Sicilian Defense. A father might have helped."

Isaac grew restless under his brother's scrutiny; he hadn't come to argue over the existence of Joel. And why should he have to be ashamed of ancient skills? Isaac lost his prowess in chess twenty-five years ago. He turned policeman in the reception room, beginning to probe his baby brother.

"Where's Marilyn? I know all about her moves. She visits you here. She jumps in and out of mama's hospital room. Leo, tell me who's putting her up? She's too particular to hide in a garbage can. Somebody's been keeping her day and night."

"I can't say."

73

"Can't, Leo? I don't like that word. Are you shielding her from me? Remember where your privileges come from. I'm not blind. The jailors let you sneak uptown to Bellevue. Call it kindness, Leo, but I'm the one who put the idea into their heads. Not for your sake. It's for mama. You're her special boy. I didn't want her to wake up in a stinking hospital without you around. Now tell me who the bastard is, the fuck who's got my girl? Name him for me."

"Isaac, go to hell."

Isaac could have throttled Leo without wrinkling his career. With the First Dep behind him, the Chief had the right to bluster with impunity. Leo's devotion to Marilyn gnawed at him. The Chief was a little jealous. Forty years I fight his battles, Isaac said to himself, and he picks Marilyn over me. Isaac's love for his brother was mingled with a kind of criminality; fondness could turn to bile in a matter of seconds. The Sidels were a bitter crew.

"Leo, you're taking advantage of me. There are tiny pricks and cunts out there who are looking to murder us. They got to Sophie. It won't happen again. But don't expect me to pamper you. I want your ass out of this jail. I'll stroke the Commissioner of Corrections if I have to. I'll fix it with your wife. Mama shouldn't have to be in a room with strangers. You stay with her until I find those freaks. Leo, I give you three days. Then I'm going to tear the jail apart."

Isaac moved across the room with hops of his broad neck. The guards peeked in. They sidled up to Leo, surrounding him with sheepish looks. "Pinochle, Leo? We have four hands today. We're ready to lose."

Leo still had the shivers, but he wouldn't disappoint the guards. "Gentlemen, I'll deal first." The guards searched for folding chairs. Leo tucked in the corners of the deck. He was hoping pinochle would save these men. Melding flushes and marriages might ease down their terror of the Chief.

The guards shivered as fast as Leo. They fumbled with the deck, throwing cards away. They couldn't auction off their marriages, or bid for trumps. Isaac had murdered their afternoon.

7.

─────────

THE FBI man wouldn't leave Isaac alone. He had his own pillow at Headquarters, and he carried it in and out of Isaac's office. Newgate adored the Chief. Jumping from Bethesda, Maryland, into a universe of Jews, Irishmen, and black detectives, he wanted Isaac to understand that he wasn't an ordinary Episcopalian. He claimed to be part Cherokee. Isaac's men sniggered at this bit of exoticism; the threat of Indian blood couldn't bring Newgate closer to them. He was made of straw, a Maryland idiot who stole words out of Isaac's mouth. He couldn't impress them with his talk of "burying" Amerigo Genussa and "sinking" Mulberry Street. Italians might be out of fashion in a year, and the FBI would be climbing trees for black militants and Puerto Rican nationalists.

Newgate squirmed on his pillow after a white nigger arrived in Isaac's office, a white nigger in a blue suede suit. He had never come across such a weird creature in his life with the FBI. It was Wadsworth, the albino from Forty-second Street, hiding his face from the sun in Isaac's windows. Only Isaac could comprehend Wadsworth's sacrifice: the albino wouldn't have exposed himself to the ruinous effects of daylight unless he had something important to deliver.

Barney Rosenblatt interrupted him. The Chief of Detectives blundered into Isaac's rooms, his suspenders forking with irritation. He wouldn't address a nigger bundled in blue suede. So he pretended Wadsworth was invisible, and he carped at Isaac. "Are you crazy? You bring a clown to Headquarters? Couldn't you negotiate with him someplace else? You'll give the PC a shit fit. Gloms like that leave an odor. Isaac, he'll scare the pants off my men."

"Eat it, Cowboy," Wadsworth said, picking dust off his sleeve.

Barney lunged at Wadsworth without taking his eyes away from Isaac.

"Out," Isaac said. "This man's registered to me. You do him any harm, and I'll collar you so fast your tongue will fall off."

Barney glowered behind his suspenders, at Wadsworth, Isaac, and Newgate. "Isaac, take the cotton out of your ears. This is Barney Rosenblatt, remember? I'm not Manfred Coen. You won't have a piece of wood left in your office, Isaac, if you come down on me."

"Pistols, Barney, is that what you want? Come, we'll have a shoot-out in the hall."

"Isaac, don't be wise." And he trudged out, the pearl handle of his Colt wobbling like a nasty stick in his pocket. Wadsworth didn't smirk; he had no interest in Barney Rosenblatt. He could piss on the walls at Headquarters, dangle his prick in front of any commissioner. Wadsworth was immune from arrest. If the burglary squad caught him napping on a fire escape, or prowling in a shoe store after midnight, they had to let him go. He belonged to Isaac and the First Dep. Wadsworth had once been a practicing arsonist. Now he was semi-retired. Not even the First Dep could rescue him if a baby died in one of his fires. So he abandoned his career as a "torch" under instructions from Isaac. He burned only vacant buildings and parking lots. "I'm sorry to cause you trouble," he said, having to nod at Isaac around Newgate's head.

"You're no trouble to me, Wads. Would you like a cherry coke?"

"Isaac, we don't have time for beverages. I think I found a lollipop for you."

"Where?" Isaac said, the hump in his neck refusing to rise with Newgate around.

"At a hospital in Corona."

Isaac rubbed his nose. "Corona? Why Corona?"

"Isaac, who knows? My uncle Quentin works in the emergency room. A kid crawls in with broken arms and legs. But there aint a scratch on the rest of his body. My uncle's not a dope. That's the mark of the landlord, Amerigo Genussa."

"What kind of kid? White or black?" Isaac said, trying to throw off the FBI man.

"Isaac, you can see for yourself."

Isaac rounded up his chauffeur Brodsky, Pimloe, his deputy whip, and his angel, Manfred Coen. Newgate began to whine. "Take me, Isaac. I'll drop a portable lab right into the kid's bed. You can tape him, fingerprint him, test his urine and his blood."

Isaac couldn't deny Newgate without creating a stink: the

79

FBI man might blab to Barney Rosenblatt. "Come," Isaac said, "but leave your lab at home." The FBI's could pull fingerprints and semen stains out of the ground with their magic laboratories. But it was never the print you needed, and the semen usually came from cats and dogs.

Brodsky telephoned for the First Dep's sedan. He marched with Isaac, Pimloe, Newgate, and Coen to the ramp in back of Headquarters. They crossed the Manhattan Bridge, Newgate marveling at the enormity of Brooklyn, which, he believed, could swallow the whole of Maryland. Brodsky was happiest with Isaac in the car. Coen annoyed him. The chauffeur despised pretty boys. Coen was the one Isaac lent to the Bureau of Special Services when an ambassador's wife grew restless in New York. Women stuck to Blue Eyes. He was the Department's prime stud. Isaac could populate the city with white niggers, Puerto Rican stoolies, and beautiful wooden-headed boys.

A dumb Maryland Cherokee like Newgate could only come alive by touching Isaac's sleeve. Isaac taught him how to sniff. He would plant evidence in your shoe, blackmail your sister, force Coen to romance your mother or your wife, until you could do nothing but cry out your guilt. This was Isaac the Pure, who didn't waste his scruples on a thief.

They arrived at St. Bartholomew's, a dinky hospital off Corona Avenue. The hospital couldn't accommodate big police cars. Brodsky found a parking spot across the street. Wadsworth had no badge to show the hospital clerks, so he walked behind Isaac, with long, pinched lines developing in the suede. The five of them burrowed into the main ward, past nurses, orderlies, and patients in rumpled gowns. Isaac was looking for a boy in traction, with his arms and legs in the air. The search became futile. They caught an old man pissing behind a screen. The man threw a pill bottle at Isaac; it struck Newgate over the eye. Isaac closed the screen.

Wadsworth led him to a boy with plaster mittens on his hands and feet; none of the mittens extended beyond the ankle or wrist. The boy was Chinese.

Coen didn't have to stare too hard; it was the boy who jumped on his chest at the Jewish youth center. He couldn't decide what to tell Isaac. The Chief didn't need prods from Coen. He examined the identification card attached to the bed: Stanley Chin didn't have an address; his age was listed as sixteen and a half. The evenness of the mittens disturbed Isaac. He couldn't be sure this was Amerigo's work. The landlord's hired goons wouldn't have restricted themselves to cracking fingers and toes. They didn't have that much finesse. The boy should have been bent at the elbows, or suffered a broken knee.

Isaac came up to the bed. His voice wasn't harsh. "Stanley Chin, do you know me?"

The boy said nothing; he watched Coen and the albino in blue.

The Chief brushed against the bed's high, criblike gate. "I'm Isaac Sidel."

The boy pushed air through his nose and wiggled his teeth against his bottom lip. Did I collar the boy's father, Isaac wondered, did I bite his family in some horrible way? He couldn't remember capturing any Chinamen in the last five or ten years.

"Why's Amerigo Genussa after you?" Newgate screamed at the boy. Isaac told him to get back. He promised to kick Newgate past the Rockaways if he interfered again.

"Stanley, tell me where your school is? Brooklyn? Queens? The Bronx?"

Wadsworth whispered to Isaac. "The kid goes to Seward Park. My uncle Quentin got that much out of him." Then he moved behind Coen. Wadsworth was getting jumpy in the hospital. A white glare came off the walls. He couldn't function without the buzzing of a movie screen. He was addicted to technicolor and dust on his face. He'd have to beg Isaac to ship him home pretty soon.

Isaac sensed the slithering motion under the suede. But he couldn't free Wadsworth until he pressed the Chinese boy.

"Stanley, did you know I went to Seward Park? I graduated in 1946. No lie. I spoke at the school a few months ago. Do you remember that?"

The boy wouldn't respond to Isaac; he rubbed the mittens on his feet while scrutinizing Wadsworth's pink eyes and colorless hair. The albino had bewitched him. Brodsky nudged Isaac on the wrist. "Chief, you'll never make this kid trading school stories. Ask me to step on his fingers, or let Manfred kiss him in the mouth."

Isaac didn't have the chance to scold Brodsky. The head nurse, an enormous black woman with a pound of starch in her midriff and her sleeves, descended upon all five of them. "What the hell do you mean busting in here without my permission?"

Brodsky answered her. "Lady, this is Chief Sidel of the First Deputy's office. He goes where he wants."

"Not in this hospital, fat man." She turned on Wadsworth. "Who the hell are you?"

The starch bristled in Wadsworth's eye, confounding him. He squeezed between Brodsky and the FBI man. Newgate fished for some identification. "Madam, I'm with the FBI."

"Jesus God," she said. "How did you lunatics get inside the door?"

Newgate's Cherokee blood bleached his nose red. "Nurse, you can check me out. I'm Amos Newgate of the Manhattan bureau."

"Sure," the woman said. "And I'm Mother Goose." She hovered over Newgate, her midriff buckling against her breast pocket. "That boy's hurt. He don't need crap from you."

Isaac would have liked to borrow this nurse; she might hold Barney Rosenblatt away from his door. Pimloe was strangely quiet. The deputy whip usually fronted for Isaac, shagging different pests off Isaac's back. Pimloe had to be in love, so Isaac mollified the nurse. "Mrs. Garden," he said, reading the name tag on her starched chest. "You're right to worry about Stanley Chin. He's your patient, and we're intruders in your ward. But we believe he's been beating up old women and destroying grocery stores. I'm leaving two of my officers here. They won't touch Stanley, I promise."

He herded Wadsworth, Newgate, and the First Deputy men out of the ward. He stationed Brodsky in the hall. "Whoever visits the kid gets a tap from you. I don't care if it's an army of midgets. Find out who they are."

"Isaac, should I stay with him?" Coen said, his cheeks slackening with drowsy lines.

"No, I want Pimloe. . . . Herbert, find the resident on this floor. Tell him to keep his bitches out of our hair."

Newgate elected to remain at the hospital. Pimloe seemed morose. "Isaac, who's gonna drive you out of Brooklyn? Wadsworth can't take the wheel."

"Coen will drive."

Brodsky's lips sank with contempt. "Chief, he doesn't know north from south. He'll lead you into the ocean. You'll drown with Coen."

"Wadsworth will save me," Isaac said, anxious to disappear from the hospital. The Chief had an errand to do. He sat with Wadsworth and Coen on the First Dep's wide front seat. Coen was hunched against the upholstery. Wadsworth kept his hands under his thighs until he had a crisp view of Manhattan. Brooklyn was a meager island in Wadsworth's head. It didn't have the proportions of a solid world. In Brooklyn the ground could sink.

Coen dropped Isaac at the Essex Street houses. Wadsworth tried to jump out of the car. Isaac was reluctant to grab some suede. He blocked Wadsworth with a knee. "You'll offend my man if you don't sit."

Wadsworth seemed afraid to sit alone with Blue Eyes. Deep colors made him crazy. The albino convinced himself that a blue-eyed Jew could only be a witch.

Isaac was in the mood for old boyfriends. Stanley Chin had thrown him back to Seward Park. The Chief scrambled for Mordecai and Philip, recollecting conversations on the roofs, fistfights over Trotsky and Stalin, chess tournaments that ruined Mordecai's appetite and made Isaac cockeyed for a week, as Philip dazzled them first with a strange opening and clubbed them over the head with his bishops and his rooks. Isaac had been fond of Mordecai, nothing more. Philip was his rival. He couldn't touch Philip in chess, or harm his defense of Trotsky's beautiful face. Isaac had always been a creaking Stalinist.

It was aggravation over Philip that caused him to abandon chess. Isaac studied the masters, absorbed the fierce play of his three gods, Morphy, Steinitz, and Alekhine, but Philip overshot all of Isaac's theories with his rough knowledge of the board; Philip moved with a crazy, internal music that contradicted Isaac's chess books. And Isaac fell to brooding. His three gods had befouled themselves. Morphy, an American boy, once the shrewdest player in the world, drifted into voyeurism during the last years of his life; he would peep out of a closet dressed in women's clothes. Steinitz, a Jewish midget from Prague, a man with spindly knees who revolutionized chess by discovering the patterns of opening play, died unloved in a beggar's grave on Ward's Island. Alekhine, the Russian genius, fled his country to play master chess throughout Europe and South America in a state of constant drunkenness, pissing on the trousers of an opponent, retching over chess clocks, and becoming the champion and sainted fool of Nazi Germany.

Philip himself went "blind" at twenty-four, lost his feel of the pieces, neglected to safeguard his king, grew restless at the board, and dropped out of tournaments. Philip became a businessman, selling lightbulbs and toilet articles to East Side stores, a husband, a father, and a recluse. His family life wasn't so different from Isaac's; both of them had stray children. Philip's boy was a stubborn genius of fifteen who could clobber his father at chess since the age of nine. Isaac decided to chat with Philip and interview the boy; he was hungry for news of Seward Park. Maybe the boy could enlighten him about Stanley's gang, and Isaac could also cry to Philip about his missing daughter, Marilyn the Wild.

One of the housing cops recognized Isaac in front of Philip's building. The cop was slightly lame, and the pieces of his uniform didn't seem to fit his body. "Chief Isaac," he shouted, "if you're shopping around for the lollipop freaks, try a new project. I control this house. Those bandits wouldn't mess with me."

"It's a social call," Isaac muttered. "I'm visiting Philip Weil."

He rode up to Philip's door. The buzzer wouldn't work, and he had to keep knocking until his fist went dead. "Philip, it's me . . . Isaac." The door opened for him. He couldn't get in without hunching himself around Philip's back. "Mordecai says you've been asking for me . . . Philip, what's the matter?"

Isaac could pull Mordecai by the nose, pluck Mordecai's daughter out of a pimp's garbage can, but he couldn't get near Philip. Philip didn't have stubble on his cheek, or the symptoms of a decayed chess master. He wore an impeccable shirt with buttons made of elephant bone and a collar strengthened with metal clips. Isaac couldn't begrudge the crease in Philip's trousers, or the neat fall of his cuffs. Philip was a stay-at-home who dressed to kill.

He'd kept his boyishness. He hadn't succumbed to Mordecai's slow fattening, or Isaac's accumulation of hard flesh. His persistent love of Trotsky and his old mania for chess must have protected him from the most common ravages. Philip lived in a closed box.

He made coffee for Isaac and himself that nearly burned Isaac's tongue. Isaac couldn't believe a man would drink such bitter stuff. He dreamed of cappuccinos at the Garibaldi social

club. "What's your problem, Philip? I should have come before . . . three little bastards hurt my mother, and they've been
on my mind."

Philip had a disturbance in his collar, a slight, nagging
twitch that may have spread from a bone behind his ears. "We
got lucky," Isaac said, his eyes on the turbulent collar. "I
think we caught one of them. A Chinese boy. Philip, imagine
this. He goes to Seward Park."

"I know. It's Stanley Chin."

Philip held the collar down with his thumb. Isaac was look-
ing mean. "Who told you that? Philip, did you fly in from
Corona this morning? Are you a patron of St. Bartholomew's?
Have you been blowing through the wards?"

"No. Rupert's with the gang. He's their leader."

A shudder ripped from Isaac's jaw, putting dark creases in
his neck. Philip's boy was a lollipop. Isaac grabbed for the
buttons on Philip's shirt. "You fucking shit, is that why
you've been sending kites to me from Mordecai?" The buttons sprang from Philip, and Isaac squeezed elephant bone
in his fist. "Philip, if my mother dies, I'll give you a permanent
earache. Crippling isn't good enough. They'll bury you with
pawns in your eyes. You'll have all the time in the world for
chess."

Philip didn't shiver with Isaac breathing over him. "Isaac,
I couldn't tell you direct. . . . I was paralyzed. I hoped you'd
come to me. I thought it was a local craziness, something he'd
get over quick. Raiding stores in the neighborhood. For what
purpose? When I heard what he did to your mother, I saw
it was too late. Isaac, nobody escapes you for very long. I've
been waiting for you to kill me, Isaac."

Isaac threw the buttons on the floor.

"What the fuck are you talking about? Philip, I'm not going to be your avenging angel. You'll suffer on your own. Give me facts. I don't want your lousy opinions. Why does Rupert hate me?"

"Isaac, I've never said a bad word about you to him."

"Maybe that's the problem. Philip, who's the cunt? The girl who runs with Stanley and Rupert."

"That's Esther Rose."

"Where does she live?"

"Isaac, she lives in the streets. Esther doesn't have a home. She used to belong to the Jewish Defense League. They kicked her out, I'm pretty sure. She was too crazy for them."

"A JDL girl? Rupert must keep a photograph of the little cunt. Where's his room?"

Philip took him into a room cluttered with pamphlets, cigar boxes, chess boards with broken spines, ping-pong bats with scars in their rubber flesh, posters advertising nudist colonies, backgammon, and guerrilla warfare, all sitting on a mound of books that hid Rupert's dresser, Rupert's closet, Rupert's lamp, and Rupert's bed. Isaac searched through the mess, up to his knees in books. He juggled a ping-pong bat, muttering hard. "Rupert ought to play with my man Coen. Coen's a whiz. Coen could seduce a polar bear with his strokes." He found a stash of photographs in one of the cigar boxes. "Is that her?" he said, pointing to a girl with frizzy hair, full bosoms, and big brown eyes.

"Yes, that's Esther."

Isaac stuffed the photograph into his pocket. Then he stole Rupert's junior-high-school graduation picture (the genius was frowning under a mortarboard hat) from a hook on the wall.

The glass in the frame began to splinter as Isaac extracted the photograph.

"Where's Rupert now?"

"Isaac, he hasn't been home in a couple of weeks. He's with Esther, that much I know."

"Philip, if you catch him, don't let him out of your sight. He's offended the biggest social club on Mulberry Street with his tactics. The Garibaldis are eager to break his shins. Philip, bring him to me."

"They won't hurt him at the stationhouse, will they, Isaac? . . . he's a baby, fifteen."

"Philip, I'd push him out a window, that boy wonder of yours, but I need him to sing. None of my men will lay a hand on him."

Isaac called St. Bartholomew's from a phone booth in the street. "Inspector Pimloe," he growled to the hospital receptionist. "Gimme Inspector Pimloe." The receptionist growled back. There weren't any Pimloes registered at the hospital. "Lady, don't cause trouble. He should be roaming in the halls. Page him for me . . . tell him Isaac says he better get his ass on the wire."

Isaac heard a sigh, and the clunking of shoes. Brodsky took the call. "Boss, it's me."

"Brodsky, jump on somebody else's wire. I asked for Pimloe, not you."

"Pimloe disappeared. Maybe he's cooping in the basement. Who knows? . . . boss, we're up shit's creek."

"Why?" Isaac said, glaring with his teeth. "Has Stanley Chin bought wings for himself? Did he tie up that nigger nurse with his bandages and flap right out of the ward?"

"Isaac, Cowboy's here."

Isaac hissed into the phone. "You dummy, how did he find you?"

"Isaac, he took me by surprise. His leather boys climbed all over me. He brought an army to the hospital. Shotguns and everything. Newgate must have snitched. Go trust the FBI!"

"Forget about Newgate. Pimloe's the man."

"Isaac, are you crazy? Pimloe works for you."

"But he's also taking care of himself. He thinks Barney Rosenblatt's armpit is the hottest place in New York City. Brodsky, use your head. It's Pimloe. It couldn't have been anybody else. Now what's Cowboy up to?"

"He's shoving us out of the picture, Isaac. You know Cowboy. He's a hog. The Chinaman is immobilized, right? So Barney kidnaps two assistant DAs, brings his camera, takes Polaroid shots of the kid, fingerprints him with his own fingerprint board, and makes a bedside arrest."

"Is Barney flaking kids these days? What the fuck does he have on Stanley Chin? Did he stick a ski mask under Stanley's pillow, or what?"

"Isaac, you can't worry him. Barney says he can produce a horde of Chinese grocers who'll swear on their lives that Stanley ripped them off. A judge is coming down tomorrow to arraign the kid."

"Tell me one thing. How did he get around the nigger nurse?"

"He didn't have to. His leather boys stuffed a shotgun in her blouse and barricaded her behind her desk."

It was idiotic to hound Brodsky for Cowboy's attack on St. Bartholomew's. Isaac hung up. He couldn't outgun the Chief of Detectives. Cowboy would yap to the Chief Inspector, the

Chief Inspector would mumble to the PC, the PC would invite the First Dep into his private elevator, and the First Dep, who couldn't divorce himself from the Irish Mafia at Headquarters, would get back to Isaac. Isaac was cooked. He'd have to cooperate with Cowboy's investigation. He couldn't even hide his photographs of Rupert and Esther Rose. The credit would go to Cowboy. He'd set up a command post inside the hospital, with "crows" on every floor.

The Chief had one alternative. He could steal the boy out of St. Bartholomew's with the help of Brodsky and Coen, and keep him in a cellar. Then Cowboy would fall from grace. But Isaac risked internecine warfare at Headquarters. He'd have to match his "angels" against Barney's "crows." The First Dep had a cancer in his throat. How long could he stay with Isaac? The Irish chiefs preferred Barney Rosenblatt. Cowboy wouldn't break ranks. He was willing to destroy any detective the PC disliked. Isaac had too much rapport with the cops in the street. He trafficked with Puerto Ricans and milk-white spades. His stoolpigeons were loyal to nobody but him. Isaac endangered the calm at Headquarters. The Irish chiefs were suspicious of him.

He waited for a Checker cab. Isaac was particular how he rode uptown. He wanted to sulk in a fat leather seat. He went to Coen. Coen would soften his misery with hot tea and a game of checkers. Isaac wouldn't play chess with Blue Eyes. Chess brought out the Chief's ferociousness, his yen for bullying weak bishops and a ragged line of pawns, and Isaac preferred not to reveal this to Coen. He had less of an appetite for checkers. He could execute double and triple jumps without relishing his victories. And Coen didn't seem to care who would win or lose.

Isaac kept away from the fire escape. He didn't have enough gusto today to climb in Coen's window. He was fond of visiting Blue Eyes at all hours. He tried Coen's doorbell. The Chief had trained ears; he heard swishing feet behind the door. "Manfred, let me in." No bolts moved. So he picked Coen's lock. "Manfred, what's doing?" He found Marilyn in Coen's foyer. She was glinting at him out of merciless eyes, with puffs on her face that had turned solid green.

Isaac backed away. He couldn't remember the last time he had trembles in his arms and knees. "I should have figured you'd be with Coen. That boy has a good heart. He'll take in anybody. Who marked up your cheeks? It wasn't Manfred."

Marilyn realized what her father might do to that old boyfriend of hers from Inwood Park. Isaac was liable to make a corpse out of Brian Connell, or destroy him in a more subtle way: he could pull Brian out of his stationhouse in the name of the First Dep and bounce him through all five boroughs until the boy lost his mind from dizziness and fatigue. Marilyn swore she'd been mugged. She knew about her father's passion for details, his eye for inconsistencies. She had to invent a full scenario for him.

"Where did it happen?"

"Midtown," she said.

"East or west?"

"Isaac, will you stop bothering me, for Christ's sake. I suppose you keep a file on every mugger in Manhattan."

She had her mother's Irish temper, that crisp, beautiful frown of Kathleen's.

"Can't you call me dad?"

"Oh God," she said. "Are we going to start that all over again? Everybody calls you Isaac. Why should I be different?"

Isaac felt his strength coming back. His fingers began to claw. "Pack your bags. You're moving in with me."

"Bullshit."

He could have dragged her to his flat on Rivington Street, made the bumps in her face go from green to pure violet, but he didn't. He would take her from Blue Eyes by persuasion alone, and he would find her no more architects to marry. The girl was miserable in a married state. She scattered husbands around her, fell from man to man. Isaac would tolerate the itch in her thighs. But she couldn't have Coen. He didn't want her craziness with Blue Eyes to follow him into Headquarters. Coen belonged to him.

"Marilyn, if you stay, I'm staying too. Manfred can fix us hot chocolate . . . he can lull us to sleep in separate rooms. We'll keep a chart on the wall about who bathes first. Manfred must be good at scrubbing backs. You understand me, Marilyn? I'm not going without you."

"Isaac, how did you ever get to be such a son-of-a-bitch?"

"It took learning," he said. "Now pack up."

She didn't prepare to leave. She watched the pinched line under Isaac's nose, pitying her father's enemies and friends; nobody could ride over Isaac.

"Marilyn, if he sees us together, he'll be the one to suffer, not you . . . don't make me bury Coen. I can turn him into a glorified clerk. Would you like him to file cards in a commissioner's basement for the rest of his life? Then cooperate with me."

"You wouldn't," she said. "You can't get by without Coen."

"I'll teach myself. Marilyn, don't misjudge your old father. Affection means nothing in my business. I'd cripple Manfred if it would take me where I have to go."

93

"Daddy Isaac," she said, with her nostrils smoking, "you don't have to tell me that." And she located her underwear, those mesh panties of hers, in yellow, red, and blue, and stuffed them into her suitcase. She flung a sweater at Isaac. "Fold it, for Christ's sake. How many hands do I have?"

"Should I leave a note for Manfred?"

"No. He'll figure out the plot. Who else would bother to kidnap me?"

Suddenly Isaac turned shy. He couldn't adjust to victories over his daughter. "Marilyn, you can still invite him down to my place. . . . I didn't say you have to avoid him altogether."

"Isaac, drop dead."

She bit her lip to keep from crying. Isaac saw the blood. He was too timid to swipe at the blood with his handkerchief. He could thank Kathleen's bloody Jesus he didn't have another child. Two Marilyns would have wrecked him. He'd rather duel with Barney Rosenblatt outside the PC's office than contemplate his skinny daughter. Isaac was a wretched man. He couldn't tuck away his love for Marilyn. She was part of his own thick flesh. Her shoulders came together, and she began to cry with little blubbering noises that tore into Isaac's throat. He touched her hair with a finger. She didn't move. He held her in a bearish grip. "Baby, it'll be all right."

They went down Coen's stairs, with Isaac managing the suitcase, and clutching Marilyn with one hand. He would have killed for the right to hold his daughter. Rupert, Stanley, and St. Bartholomew's tumbled out of his head.

Part Two

———————

8

"M<small>R</small>. Weil, Mr. Philip Weil."

The reporter crouched under Philip's doorknob, his eye against the keyhole, waiting for the darkness to subside. He was a clever young man, fresh out of journalism school, with a flair for identifying the peccadilloes of his own generation. He'd received encouragement from a fistful of magazines: nothing firm, nothing really bankable, but if he could interview the father of Rupert Weil, the monster with baby fat on his chin, no magazine could deny him for long. His thighs burned. He wasn't used to crouching so much. And the blackness in the keyhole had smogged his eye.

"I've got fifty dollars for you, Mr. Weil . . . conversation money," he said, with a torn dollar bill and two subway tokens in his pocket. He would lure the monster's father out, this recluse, this failed chess player, this Essex Street clown who had once been the friend of the great Isaac Sidel, or bluff his way into the apartment. "You're not talking to a sharp, Mr. Weil. I would never degrade your boy. This is Tony Brill, the journalist. I have connections, Mr. Weil. . . . I can cream the police and make Rupert come out like a hero . . . it's up to you."

Philip was hiding in the kitchen, immune to the imprecations of Tony Brill. He wouldn't sell Rupert's story, no matter what figure the journalist could name. He'd been besieged with phone calls, telegrams, knocks on his door. The newspapers had Rupert's face smeared in their centerfolds, with captions about derangement and banditry. The Lollipop Gang and the Urban Blitz. Rupert Weil, Teenage Ghoul. Esther Rose, Temptress, Evil Saint, Dropout from the JDL, and Mama to the Lollipops. And Stanley Chin, Hong Kong Bully Boy. A fat detective, Cowboy Rosenblatt, haunted Philip's television screen. Cowboy spit warnings to potential lollipops from Stanley's hospital bed, which had been turned into a compact prison, and he hogged every channel with profiles of Rupert and Esther Rose, self-congratulations, and anecdotes about his police career. Philip couldn't find Isaac in any of the programs and news reports featuring Cowboy Rosenblatt; none of the detectives who badgered him over the phone came from Isaac's office.

When soft-spoken men from the District Attorney's office tried to scare information out of him, Philip would bray into the telephone, "I'll talk to Isaac and nobody else." But Isaac wouldn't come. The Chief had disappeared from Philip's life after a single visit. And Philip was left alone to slink in his kitchen and contemplate the madnesses of his boy.

Philip closed his eyes; he wanted to shake off the briny calculations in his skull. Thinking could ruin him, rub his nose into the painted squares of a chessboard. He wasn't able to kill the barking outside his door. The moment he surrendered to these noises and slumped against the wall, the barking had a definite appeal: it drew him out of the kitchen. The yelps were growing familiar. He pressed his ear to the door.

"Papa, let me in."

"Rupert?" he said, struggling with the chain guard. Even if Tony Brill were some kind of sound magician, how could he have known the exact tremors of Rupert's voice? Philip put his hand out the door, clutched a jacket, and hauled Rupert inside. The fat cheeks were gone. Rupert looked emaciated. He wore the jacket of a housing cop. This was his only disguise. With a hard pull, the jacket could have reached to his ankles. Bound in dark, billowing cloth, Rupert had no fists, no throat, no chest. Philip unraveled him. Except for old, disheveled sneakers and pants, he was naked under the jacket, the first manly hairs, almost blond, sprouting over his nipples. A squeal escaped from Philip's throat; his mad love for the boy turned to an incredible rage. He had Rupert's ear in his fingers. He would have gone for a nose. Rupert knocked him down. Philip sat with his knees in his chest. A simple push had stunned him, not a wicked blow.

"Papa, don't touch my ear again. I'm too old for that."

Rupert didn't sneer; he hugged Philip under the arms and straightened Philip's knees. He was delicate with his father, picking him up. Then he walked into the kitchen. Philip had to stare at his back; half of Rupert was inside the refrigerator. He tore into the flesh of a tomato, marking the refrigerator walls with red spit. He swallowed sour pickles. He crammed his face into a container of cottage cheese. Philip was appalled by his son's appetite. He'd never encountered a boy with such greedy jaws. Rupert was all tongue and teeth. Philip had lost his way with him. How could he confront this child of his, who was trying to shove the universe into his mouth?

"Rupert, did you notice a journalist in the hall, a man named Brill?"

Rupert emerged from the refrigerator, cottage cheese falling from his eyebrows. "The fatass in the trench coat? He saluted me."

"But he saw you standing by the door."

"So what? What can he do, papa? Let him blab to Isaac. Who gives a shit."

"Isaac was here," Philip declared with a pull of his shoulder, as Rupert dove into the cottage cheese again. "I said Isaac was here."

Rupert mumbled with his lips inside the container. "I heard you, papa." He came up for air, flicking cheese off his nose. "Why did you supply him with pictures of Esther and me?"

"Rupert, he would have torn out the walls. Isaac doesn't give you much room to breathe. But he wants to help. . . . Rupert, has he done bad things to you?"

"Papa, you're a woodenhead. Isaac's been fucking you blind. You and Mordecai can't stop paying homage to him. He's your king. At least Mordecai gets some satisfaction. He brags about Isaac. He talks about the Jewish god who presides over New York City, the kosher detective who can solve any crime. And you, papa? You eat your liver without saying a word. Where's your terrain? Isaac's left you his droppings. He's made you prince of the Essex Street project. You walk around in your three good shirts wishing you were Isaac."

"That's crazy," Philip said. "I don't envy his success."

Rupert sucked with wolfish teeth. "Success, papa? That's it. Success to do what? Blow people away? To prance in front of Puerto Ricans and poor Jews. Isaac shits in peace because he has his worshipers and his props. He can enter any church or playground on both sides of the Bowery and be guaranteed a smile. Even the horseradish man bows to Isaac. Papa, if you could learn to despise him, he'd run uptown with a handkerchief over his ears. He'd disintegrate. He'd cry in Riverdale."

Rupert scooped up his jacket off the floor and began stuffing the pockets with food. After scavenging his father's refrigerator, he climbed into the jacket and waddled to the door. The pockets hung below his knees.

"I'll hide you," Philip said. "You can stay here."

"What happens when Isaac sweeps under the bed?"

"He'll find twenty years of dust, and a few missing pawns."

"Thanks, papa, but I have to go." Rupert pulled up his sleeves so he could hug his father. Then he rushed into the hall, jars smacking in his pockets. Tony Brill appeared from behind a fire door. "That's him, Mr. Weil, isn't it? Rupert himself. I can spot a fugitive by his walk."

Tony Brill didn't go after Rupert. He lunged at Philip's door. Philip locked him out. "I can save him, Mr. Weil . . . trust me."

Philip returned to the kitchen, ignoring the babble. He was interested in weather reports. Did the television predict snow? Rupert would catch pneumonia in his sneakers. Philip shouldn't have let him out of the house without a proper undershirt. The boy had no mind for cold weather. His thumbs would have to freeze before the idea of frostbite entered his head. How could Philip signal to him? Should he fly scarves from his fire escape? He laughed bitterly at his own incompetence. He had just enough energy in him to become a father. His wife, a Russian girl with handsome bosoms and a flat behind, stared him in the eye for eleven years and ran away before Rupert was six. Sonia, the Stalinist, must have found other causes than a man who would die for Trotsky and chess and a boy who looked more like her husband than herself. She was supposed to be in Oregon, living with a band of apple pickers, a gray-haired Russian lady.

Philip berated himself. A father should have the right to make a prisoner of his son, if only for a little while. He meant to jab the boy with questions, brutal questions, not a dialectical checklist that would give Rupert the chance to invent a shabby scheme, a rationale for frightening old grocers and sending Isaac's mother to Bellevue. But Philip was powerless; his own questions would glance off Rupert and bite Philip behind the ears. If Rupert had a dybbuk in him, a demon sucking at his intestines, who put it there? Such a dybbuk could only be passed from father to son. The violence Philip had done to his body, the gnawing of his own limbs, the self-lacerations that came a nibble at a time, the rot of living indoors, the poison of chess formulas, degrees of slaughter acted out on a board, the insane fondling of wooden men, pawns, bishops, and kings, must have created a horrible, scratchy weasel that crept under Rupert's skin, grabbed his testicles, tightened his guts, and caused conniptions in his brain. The dybbuk was Philip. No one else.

❖

Rupert was on the run. He had to fight the weight in his pockets, the shifting, sliding bottles and jars, the wind that slapped the enormous collars of the jacket he stole out of a grubby bungalow that belonged to the housing cops. His belly gurgled from the pickles he swallowed in his father's apartment. He couldn't dash across a housing project with burgeoning pockets and also digest pickles and cottage cheese. Hiccoughs broke his miserable stride. He avoided the shoppers huddling out of the bialy factory on Grand Street with their bags of onion bread. They might have recognized him, in spite of his jacket. They would scream, splinter bialys in his face, and call for the big Jewish Chief, Isaac Sidel, or the nearest housing cop. He didn't have the patience to dodge bialys and pick onions out of his eyes. He was going to Esther Rose.

Rupert couldn't grasp all of Esther's fervors. She'd come out of a Yeshiva in Brownsville that would only accept the daughters of the Sephardim of Brooklyn. Stuck in a neighborhood of Puerto Ricans, blacks, and rough Polish Jews, it had gates on every side. The Yeshiva was impregnable. None of the Polish Jews could gain access to its prayer rooms and library. The girls were rushed in through a door in the back. They had little opportunity to examine what existed outside the Yeshiva's front wall. They understood the hypnotic candlepower of a 25-watt bulb. They could feel bannisters in the dark. They had a gift for reciting Ladino, the gibber of medieval Spanish and Hebrew that was used exclusively at this Yeshiva. The Sephardic priests who ran the school took it upon themselves to push every girl towards hysteria. The girls had to consider what worthless creatures they were. They became despondent over the largeness of their nipples, the untoward shape of their breasts, the sign of pubic hair, the bloody spots in their underpants. Nothing on this earth except the lowly female was cursed with a menstrual flow, their teachers advised them. Husbands had already been selected for the girls by a system of bartering inside their families. Only a girl with the resources of her family behind her could command a proper husband, usually twice her age.

Esther was taught the rituals of marriage at the Brownsville school for Sephardic girls, the veils she would wear, the menstrual charts she would keep to warn her husband of the exact days of her impurity. Esther had seven years of this, muttering prayers whenever she touched her nipple or her crotch by accident, dreaming of her life as a workhorse for her future husband and his family, trading pubic hairs with a sinful schoolmate, feeling razors in her womb at the onset of her periods, despising bowel movements, sweat, and the color of her urine. A month before she was scheduled to marry a merchant with hair in his nose, Esther ran away. She drifted through Brooklyn, working for the telephone company. Then she joined the JDL. Her parents, who lived in an enclave of Spagnuolos (Sephardic Jews) between Coney Island and Gravesend, included Esther in their prayers for the dead. They couldn't tolerate the existence of a daughter who would shun a marriage contract to embrace the Jewish Defense League. Zionism meant nothing to Esther's people. Israel was a place for Germans, Russians, and Poles, barbarians to most of the Sephardim, who remembered the kindness of the Moors to Spanish Jews. The ancestors of Esther Rose, mathematicians, prophets, and moneylenders, had flourished under Arabic rule; it was difficult for the south Brooklyn Sephardim to hold a legitimate grudge against Egypt and Saudi Arabia, or the Syrians and Lebanese of Atlantic Avenue.

Rupert first bumped into Esther Rose outside the Russian embassy in Manhattan half a year ago. She was carrying a placard denouncing Soviet intransigence towards the State of Israel. She harassed policemen and the citizens of Fifth Avenue, wearing an old, smelly blouse and a wraparound skirt that exposed her unwashed ankles and knees; she flew at her adversaries with uncombed hair and fingernails that had all the corrugations of a saw. Rupert couldn't take his eyes off Esther Rose. He had never known a girl who lived at such a raw edge. Esther noticed the chubby boy staring at her. She didn't bite his eyebrows. She looked beyond the pedestrian nature of fat cheeks. This wasn't a boy she could frighten with placards or a rough fingernail.

She had coffee egg creams with him at a dump on Third Avenue. He blurted his age: fifteen. She'd picked up a child (Esther was two years away from being twenty). The fat cheeks had an erudition that could touch a Yeshiva girl under her brassiere. This baby talked of Sophocles, Rabbi Akiba, St. Augustine, the Baal Shem, Robespierre, Nikolai Gogol, Hieronymus Bosch, Huey P. Newton, Prince Kropotkin, and Nicodemus of Jerusalem. He had the delirious, twitching eyes of a Sephardic priest, the sour fingers of a virgin boy. She would have climbed under the table with Rupert, licked him with coffee syrup on her tongue. The egg cream must have made him reticent. He was suspicious of lying down in a field of cockroaches and candy wrappers, under the gaze of countermen.

Esther relied on ingenuity. She picked Atlantic Avenue, where she knew of a mattress they could rent by the hour. Rupert wouldn't go. It violated his sense of purity. He brought her to an abandoned building on Norfolk Street. They undressed in the rubble, Esther's knees sinking through the floorboards. The boy was passionate with her. He fondled Esther with a sly conviction, and soon they were eating dust off one another's body. Esther was a Brooklyn girl. Norfolk Street remained a mystery to her. But she could love a building with missing staircases, rotting walls, and windows blocked with tin. She gave up the question of Palestine for Rupert's sake. She two-timed the JDL, staying near Norfolk Street to become Rupert's permanent "mama."

Rupert slinked away from his father's house, crippled by jars in his pockets. He was trying to shake that journalist, Tony Brill. He stumbled in and out of street corners, his ankles beginning to swell from the pressure of jars sliding off his hips. Esther had to jump from building to building, protecting herself from nosy people and cops of the Puerto Rican and Jewish East Side. Rupert found her on Suffolk Street. She was a choosy girl, hiding in a tenement with gargoyles near the roof, rain spouts with broken noses. He entered through a window on the ground floor, grabbing his pockets and heaving them over the sill. He could follow Esther's ascent in the building by the drawings over each set of stairs. She'd crayoned faces next to the landings, faces with swollen foreheads and frothy mouths: men and women drugged with the burden of their own heavy brains. The drawings stopped abruptly at the fourth floor. Rupert didn't have to peek any higher. "Esther," he called. "It's me."

She sat on her haunches in deep concentration, wearing a blanket, like a Brooklyn squaw (Esther depised street clothes). She was cooking something in a pot, with the Sterno can Rupert had given her. The stink coming off the pot settled under Rupert's tongue; he walked around the room biting his jacket to keep from swallowing his own poisoned spit. "What the hell are you making?" he shouted with Esther's fumes in his eyes.

"Food," she said. "Food for Isaac."

"Isaac's not a schmuck. He won't drink mud out of a pot."

"Then I'll feed it to him. I can stuff Isaac anytime."

"How?" Rupert asked. "Are you going to mail him some doctored horseradish?"

"No. I'll sneak it into his lousy Headquarters."

"Esther, Isaac's got a fortress on Centre Street. You know how many guns there are on every floor? Detectives sleep in the woodwork. You can't pee without an escort."

"So what?" she said. "I'm not going to hold Isaac's prick."

"Esther, listen to me. You haven't eaten in four days." He smacked the bulges in his pockets. "I have my father's sour pickles. I have stuffed cabbage. I have grape leaves."

"I'm not hungry."

Esther had been cold to Rupert over the past week; she blamed him for losing Stanley Chin. They'd all gone out to Corona because Manhattan was flooded with cops and gorillas from Mulberry Street. They were shrewd enough to outrun the gorillas, who seemed stranded outside Little Italy, and couldn't tell the difference between a ski mask (Esther's contribution to the gang), a wool helmet, and a winter scarf; these gorillas must have come from a warmer climate, where a sane person wouldn't think of putting a rag on his head. But the lollipops weren't so sure of the police; cops came smart and dumb, and even a dumb cop could signal Isaac with a portable radio.

Corona was Rupert's idea; he intended to plague Isaac from a fresh neighborhood. The lollipops would attack grocery stores, spit Isaac's name at their victims. But a gang of baby Chinamen had followed them out on the Queensboro line, old compatriots of Stanley Chin's from his days as a strong-arm boy for merchants and Republican politicians on Pell Street. The gang was seeking revenge; Stanley had insulted his former employers, the Pell Street Republican Club, with his raids on Chinatown as a member of the lollipops. These baby Chinamen, called the Snapping Dragons by their enemies, had no interest in Rupert and Esther Rose; they weren't out to punish a pair of round-eyed Jews. They jumped on Stanley's back outside the subway stop in Corona, wrestled him to the ground, broke every single one of his fingers and toes, while Esther screamed and dove into their ranks, and two un-occupied Dragons held Rupert by his arms. Esther forbid explanations from Rupert. With her head burrowing in the groin of a Snap Dragon, she'd heard the pop of Stanley's fingers. Rupert had come out of Corona unmarked.

She stared at his unwieldy jacket. "Take that thing off," she said. "It makes you look like a traffic cop."

Rupert obeyed her. He stood with goose bumps sprouting on his chest. He couldn't get her away from that concoction she was brewing for Isaac. His motives were simple: he wanted Esther to fuck. Rupert had a perfect right to be lascivious with her. He worshiped Esther's body, loving the damp skin of a Yeshiva girl, the exquisite bends in her shoulder, her arching wings, the salt he licked out of her navel, the swampy aromas from the underside of her knee, the scissoring of her thighs. He had touched one junior-high-school girl before Esther, felt the exaggerated pimple on this girl's chest, dry, odorless skin, and the random hairs that grew out of the hems in her underpants. But he couldn't have conceived the delicate, moist machinery of a female's parts without Esther. Rupert would have murdered the whole of Essex Street for the privilege of putting his face between Esther's legs, or fucking her until her neck throbbed with the power of her orgasm.

She would give him nothing today. Rupert understood that. Esther was punishing him for Stanley's fall. Should he break his own thumbs to please her? The denial of her body terrified him. He would have groveled on the dirty floor to suck Esther's kneecaps if he knew this might arouse her, or at least catch Esther off her guard. He stuck his hands in his armpits to keep them warm. He shivered and sulked, the goose bumps snaking up and down his spine.

Esther whipped one elbow and cast her blanket out at Rupert, drawing him into her reach. They stood belly to belly in the cold; then Esther relocated the blanket, and they descended together, with a rub of their hips, while Rupert's pants came down. They rolled on the blanket, Rupert amazed by his sudden change of luck. No matter how many times their bodies clapped, he would never fathom Esther's needs. But he didn't question the grace of sleeping with Esther. She'd grounded him in a blanket, and he was stuck with bits of wool over his ears, Esther underneath. He crept into her, loosening her thighs with a fist that hadn't quite lost its baby fat. Esther had her frenzy with Rupert's hair in her mouth. Now she lay still, watching the agitation build in his nose. Esther knew what it means when a man begins to blow air.

She brought Rupert out of her with a great squeeze of her abdominal muscles before Rupert had the chance to snort in her face (Yeshiva girls didn't believe in condoms, diaphragms, or coils). Rupert dribbled on her chest. He wasn't surly. He tried to paint her bosoms with his come, draw on Esther with a sticky finger, but she wouldn't let him. She snatched up her blanket and returned to the pot.

"I need some ammonia for the soup," she said.

Rupert put on his pants. "Why ammonia?"

"Just get some for me."

"Esther, I can't trade in pickles for cash. Who's going to give me free ammonia?"

"Steal it," she hissed into his ear. "Don't come back without my goods."

Rupert fled the building with the same bottles and jars (he'd forgotten to empty his jacket). He stumbled out into the narrow gutters of Suffolk Street, his sneakers sliding over raw stone. He hitched up his pockets and tried to remember if the Cuban grocery stores carried ammonia. He couldn't determine the nature of Esther's stew; whatever she was feeding Isaac, would it come hot or cold? A fat man in a vague, military coat cornered him on Norfolk Street. It was Tony Brill. Rupert sneered.

"Follow me, man, and I'll torture your balls. You know what I do to people. I'm Rupert Weil."

Tony Brill ran after Rupert. Soon both of them were huffing insanely for air. The journalist managed to claw three words out of his throat. "Talk to me."

They rested on opposite sides of a lamppost. Rupert extended his palm. "Cash, you fuck. Gimme all your money."

Tony Brill urged a torn dollar into Rupert's palm. "That's it. Now will you talk?"

Rupert made a fist, the dollar showing through his fingers. He had his ammonia money; he was too exhausted to steal from a grocery.

"Rupert, you can be a famous man. Tell me, do you suffer when they call you an urban bandit? What's the significance of your refusal to touch cash? Is it blood you want, not money? Will you and Esther raid stores without Stanley Chin? Are you a different kind of Robin Hood?"

"No," Rupert said. "I'm my father's boy." He pushed Tony Brill off the sidewalk and ran towards a section of grocery stores.

❖

Esther was tired of churning soup in a scummy pot; she could hear the suck of bubbles underneath the scum. Nothing but ammonia would ever quiet such a noise. She'd make Isaac swallow her soup with his ears. There was more than one way to poison a big Jewish cop. Isaac would piss blood by tomorrow. Rupert was too soft. He couldn't punish the Chief without Esther Rose.

Yeshiva girls aren't blind; she'd seen the fat on Rupert disappear. Who was gouging Rupert's cheeks? Isaac the Pure. All of Rupert's dread came from the big Jew. She'd told him. "Rupert, you love your father too much. Is it your fault he's under Isaac's thumb? Why didn't he pack years ago and move

out of Essex Street? Isaac's killing your father. Don't let him
kill you."

He'd get angry with her. "How the hell do you know so
much? Did your rabbis teach you the philosophy of Philip
Weil? My father's scared to move. You expect him to crawl
over the Brooklyn Bridge? He'd die in a strange place. Ask the
scientists. You can lose your head if you stray from where you
were born."

"We'll find him another one. When your guts shrivel, it's
too late."

"Stop talking about my father. Leave his guts alone."

It didn't offend her. She could only love an obstinate boy.
The sweat would pour from his eyebrows. The hollows in his
cheeks would curl. He was handsomer to her than Isaac's
baby, Mr. Blue Eyes. She wouldn't take down her underpants
for the prettiest cop in the world. She was particular about
the men she laid. Truck drivers, grocers, JDL boys, but no
blond detective could get on her list.

The soup in Esther's pot smelled worse than the semen of
a Williamsburg cat. The vapors were attacking her sinuses.
Esther had to get out. She grabbed for her pea coat. Her fist
burrowed into her sleeve like the skull of a groundhog, but she
wouldn't button up. The blanket dropped below her calves.
Esther didn't believe in skirts. You couldn't feel the wind on
you if your legs were muggered in cloth. She had a ski mask
balled in her pocket. She could bring terror to the neighborhood by pulling that mask over her head. Merchants would
scream, "Lollipop, lollipop," and rush to the deepest corner
of their shops. Seeing a merchant quake couldn't satisfy her
any more. The merchants had a king with curly sideburns.
Isaac the Jew. Esther swore to unhinge him.

The first time Rupert brought her into the East Side, to
Norfolk Street, Essex, Delancey, Grand, Esther had realized
the conditions of this territory. "Who's the big tit here? Tell
me the name of your rabbi."

The boy couldn't answer her. "Esther, what do you mean?"
"Somebody's been squeezing these blocks for a long time.
It's too quiet. There isn't a drop of anarchy on East Broadway.
Where's the chief?"

Rupert thought for a moment. Then he mumbled, "At
Police Headquarters." And he told her about Isaac, and Isaac's
grip over hoodlums, policy men, shopkeepers, Seward Park
High School, Ida Stutz, Mordecai, Philip, and Rupert himself.
"He stinks," Rupert said. "But nobody's willing to say it."

Esther understood. Isaac was the Moses of Clinton and
Delancey. Hadn't the idiot priests at her school shoved stories
into her face about the sanctity of patriarchs? The Jews had
more fathers than Esther could bear. An army of fathers with
a single word under their tongues: Obey. When she married,
said the priests, wouldn't her husband be like a father to her?
A father who could enjoy Esther's parts. She'd have to cleave
to her father-husband, make herself bald for him (hair on the
female scalp was a sign of degradation and lust), feed him,
fuck for him, mend his shirts, rub the pee stains out of his
skivvies, stuff her womb with male heirs.

A wife was little better than any beast of the field. She was
instructed to close her eyes and grunt when her husband
climbed on top (intercourse in all other varieties, or positions,
was immodest and perverse). He, the lord of the house, had
to fuck with the Torah in his head, while his wife suffered the
stab of her master's knees and prayed for a male child. Thank
God for menstruation, Esther figured. A wife with blood in

her drawers was unclean property. Her lord couldn't drink from her cup, or graze her with a forefinger after the first trickle. Then she had her nights and days to herself. She couldn't become pure again until she removed the wax from her ears and dipped her pink scalp into a pool of slimy water. These were the joys of a Yeshiva wife.

Esther had a solution. She could become Isaac's bride. It would be no marriage of convenience, arranged by rich uncles, with fat dowries and long trousseaus. Esther would bite away the traditional Ladino blessings. She'd construe a marriage without bridal veils and jeweled canopies as old as the Moorish occupation of Seville. There would be nothing between Esther and Isaac other than pride, venom, and a goatish itch. Bride and groom would ravage one another on their wedding night, fornicating with the energy of absolute hate. She'd tear off Isaac's nose with an early orgasm. He'd pound her kidneys with every smack of his hard, policeman's belly, and scald her groin with his steamy come. She'd suck up all the delicate glue in his eyes. Isaac would rage with his fingers over the shells of his face, ruined by the powerful flicks of Esther's tongue. The butchery would continue into the morning, when the remains of Esther and Isaac would be found in the crush of lavender wedding sheets: two well-preserved shinbones and a purple knot of blood.

Esther carried her visions into the street. Several laborers who were digging holes in the sidewalk happened to see a girl with tits peeking out of her coat. They abandoned their shovels to howl at Esther. "Sweetheart, honey, baby dear, you'll catch cold without an undershirt. Ask us, we'll block the wind for you." She stepped around the holes, refusing to change the course of her buttons. Delivery boys and retired

men from Grand Street gaped into the open pea coat and felt
a knock between their eyes: it was painful to stare at a nipple
moving in winter light. *"Cuño,"* the boys said. The old men
gave embarrassed shrugs and consoled themselves with
thoughts of a bialy and piss-colored tea.

Rupert was ten feet away. He heard none of the commotion
surrounding Esther. There were deep bumps in his forehead.
Esther didn't nudge him, or cry hello. She had too much respect for Rupert's brainstorms. He was hugging Esther's ammonia under his arm. He walked past her, oblivious to the
howling of laborers and delivery boys. Esther adored him
chubby or thin, but she was frightened of his skeletal look.
Rupe, she wanted to say. Forget about them Chinese Dragons.
Stanley won't die in Corona. It's not your fault you never
learned kung-fu. I'm not mad any more. But the sharp line of
his ears startled her, and Esther didn't say a thing.

She developed a hunger strolling on Ludlow Street. Shutting
her pea coat to confound the Puerto Rican clerks, she entered
a tiny *supermercado.* A second girl came into the market while
Esther shoved a mushy tangerine under her coat. The girl's
Irish nose and kinky Jewish hair got to Esther. *I know that
cunt.* Isaac's skinny daughter. It had to be. The cunt was living with Isaac now. Rupert and Esther had noticed her sitting
on Isaac's fire escape. Marilyn liked to bathe in cold air. They
watched her from the roofs, Esther wishing she could break
off Marilyn's kneecaps. She was less ferocious in the supermarket, having only one small urge to take out her mask and
spook Marilyn the Wild. The moist touch of tangerine skin
on her breasts calmed Esther Rose. She went about her business of swiping more fruit.

The clerks grew wise to Esther. How many *muchachas*

ranged through their market in a pregnant pea coat? They
yanked the bottom of her coat, yelling thief, thief. Tangerines,
avocado pears, and overripe green peppers plopped to the floor
of the market with an agonizing squish. Esther struck at the
clerks with a whirling elbow. "You want a slap in the balls
maybe?"

"Call the cops, man," the head clerk screamed. Then he
recognized Marilyn, who was trying to get between Esther
and the clerks. "Your father should come, Señorita Marilyn.
This muchacha needs the handcuffs and a pistola in the
mouth."

"I'll pay," Marilyn screamed into the clerk's bobbing hair-
line. She saw the foam build on Esther's lip. It was dumb to
make an arrest over avocados and green peppers. The girl was
either crazy, or starving for fruit. Marilyn grabbed a dollar
from her pocketbook. The clerks refused her money. "No, no,
Señorita Marilyn." They released Esther's coat. She stuck her
teeth near Marilyn's chin.

"Who asked you for your fucking charity?"

"Loco," the clerks whispered to themselves. Little crooks
like Esther were a common nuisance in their trade. Roaches,
ants, dogs, mice, and other predators could destroy your in-
ventory.

Marilyn didn't remain with the clerks; she followed the
track of Esther's pea coat. The two girls bumped across Grand
Street. "What's your name?" Marilyn asked.

Esther smiled. "Me? I'm Rupertina. I live in the projects.
I have eleven brothers, Miss, so help me God. My mother's
dead. My father doesn't have a tooth. He licks the gutters for
a living. Tell me, is your daddy alive?"

The girl's dire history caused Marilyn to brood. But there

was a curious edge to this Rupertina's voice. "Do you know my father? He's a police inspector. Isaac Sidel."

Esther had to hold back her pity for Marilyn the Wild. The cunt will be an orphan in twenty hours. "Miss, I never heard of any Isaac."

Esther jumped onto the sidewalk and scampered away. She wished she had a lollipop embedded in her ski mask. She could bite through the wrapper and get some colored juice on her tongue. The growls in her belly pushed her towards Suffolk Street and Rupert's sour pickles. The dudes from the Seward Park handball courts wouldn't stop pestering her. They were boys with scarves, blue sneakers, and silver posts hanging from their left ears. They had canes with points sharp enough to stab a girl's pockets. "Come on down to the playground with us, little mama. We gonna feast on you."

Esther growled at the dudes, slapping their canes off her sides. "Don't you know who I am?" she said, ready to grab a silver post and pull on a dude's ear. "I'm Isaac's daughter."

The boys retrieved their canes. "Honky Isaac?" they said. "The Papa Jew?"

"That's him."

They were suspicious. "What's the big honky's daughter doing in the street without no pants and skirt?"

"I'm coming from a rendezvous."

"What's that?" the boys demanded of her.

"A religious meeting. With a rabbi. You hold it in a swimming pool. Every month. It washes all your germs."

The dudes spread apart from Esther; she could contaminate them with her talk of rabbis, germs, and swimming pools.

Esther arrived on Suffolk Street. Rupert was waiting on the fourth floor of Esther's tenement with a bottle of ammonia.

They went into the room where Esther kept her pot. She relit the Sterno can and poured some ammonia into her soup without thanking the boy. "Pickles," she said. "Bring me a pickle."

Rupert brought over his father's jars. While Esther stirred the pot, he fed her sour pickles, grape leaves, and bits of cabbage. She stepped out of her coat, and Rupert had to squint at the wall to keep his mind off the thrust of her ass and the beautiful pull of her ribs. Esther had a frightening concentration. She'd scream at him if he tried to fuck her in the middle of mixing the soup. Rupert saw his limits. He was only the nominal head of the lollipops. The gang's spirit came from Esther. She's the one who planned their forages into the East Side. They would chop up the giant a finger at a time, attack Isaac at the peripheries, nestle in his armpits, slap his appendages down.

Rupert's eyes were burrowing into the wall when he felt a hand inside his coat. Esther had started to undress him. He didn't resist. He took her favors however they happened to come. "I still think Isaac isn't going to drink your soup so fast."

"Shut up," she said. His heart beat against the bumps in her palm. Soon they were lying in Esther's coat. This was a fragile boy, with the heartbeat of a captured bird. According to the Sephardic priests, it was sinful to fornicate with Esther on top. Fuck the priests. Esther would invent her own religion. She was in love with a boy who had watched his father nibble at himself for fifteen years. Piecemeal deaths were the ugliest. Rupert caught his father's disease. He couldn't creep out from under Isaac.

Her tongue crowded into Rupert's teeth. She heard the boy

snort. She'd have to fatten up his face. It was impossible with
Isaac around. Esther meant to win, even if she had to become
Isaac's bride. She didn't fret over it. The marriage would be
very lean.

Part Three

9.

——————

Isaac arrived at the Neptune Manor on Ocean Parkway in
ordinary clothes; he wouldn't retrieve any of his five velvet
jackets (champagne yellow, cucumber green, orange, red, and
mole gray) from his wife's apartment, up in Riverdale, for the
wedding of an old maid. Marilyn refused to come with him, so
he had to bring Coen. The "crows" from Barney Rosenblatt's
office, who sacrificed their leather pockets for Cowboy and
came in sharkskin and rich gabardine, tittered at Isaac's "date."
Coen was in the doghouse, all of them knew; he'd committed
the primary sin of romancing Marilyn Sidel.

Isaac and Coen had been put in a corner, far from the
wedding table, where Cowboy sat with his oldest daughter, his
new son-in-law (a haberdasher with rotten teeth), First
Deputy Commissioner O'Roarke, the Chief Inspector, and
the PC, together with their wives, and two young deputy

mayors, honorable men with sideburns and advanced college degrees, who felt smug in a room filled with cops. Anita Rosenblatt wore a veil that obscured a crooked nose and the long, burrowing chin of her father. The bride was thirty-two. She suffered from falling hair, the result of a nervous condition that left her with a poisoned scalp. Even Isaac, who hated Cowboy, couldn't deny the appeal Anita had in her wedding gown. She survived bald spots and imperfections in her face. Staring at the haberdasher, she had a flush that could swallow any veil, or pinch the sourness off the cheeks of an Irish commissioner.

Anita presided over the smorgasbord. The assistant district attorneys of Manhattan, Brooklyn, and Queens, standing opposite the bride, devoured enormous boats of pickled cabbage. A fountain governed by the figure of Neptune climbing out of the sea (done in silver and gold), spit lemon punch into a basin near Neptune's toes with enough force to drown a baby, or a small dog.

Isaac discovered Herbert Pimloe behind a tray of midget salamis. Only respect for Commissioner O'Roarke, the First Dep, prevented Isaac from shoving a salami down Pimloe's throat. O'Roarke was a sick man. He didn't need to be shamed by his own inspectors at a catered affair. Isaac wedged Pimloe into the salamis without a hint of malice. "Herbert, they tell me Cowboy has a new steerer."

Pimloe tried to slip outside the smorgasbord. Isaac held him in place with two fingers. Pimloe was reluctant to move. "Isaac, you can't believe everything you hear."

"Herbert, did Cowboy give you a wedding ring? Or is it an informal engagement?"

Pimloe accommodated Isaac with a toothless smile. The

veins in his ears showed red. "Chief, you shouldn't listen to the FBI."

"Herbert, how much did Cowboy promise? Half the city? Is that what it took to turn you around? Is he giving you Brooklyn, or the Bronx? Herbert, I want to know."

"Isaac, I didn't screw you, I swear."

"Pimloe, you told Cowboy where to find Stanley Chin. And don't hand me shit about Newgate. Newgate wouldn't suck Cowboy's nipples. He's got too much pride. It takes a Harvard boy."

Isaac left Pimloe to brood against the moist skins of the salamis. His anger was mostly counterfeit. The Chief couldn't blame a quiff for trying to improve himself. Herbert played the percentages. He had to figure Cowboy was a better rabbi than O'Roarke. Why should Pimloe attach his badge and his pants to a dying commissioner?

Isaac marched to the wedding table. He might bang shoulders with Barney, but he wouldn't insult the bride. He kissed Anita under the veil, wishing her a long and happy marriage in spite of the feuds at Headquarters. The veil rubbed Isaac's nose. He could feel the stiff corseting of her gown. He prayed Anita wouldn't lose her haberdasher-husband. He knew all about daughters who had a talent for wiggling away from their men. Thinking of Marilyn brought Isaac back to Coen. He'd rather have her single than see her with Blue Eyes. Coen made a perfect cop. Without brains, or ambition, he was utterly reliable. What could he offer Marilyn except those damn blue eyes?

Under the cold, rabbity gaze of the Police Commissioner and his wife, who shoveled potato salad into their mouths as they scrutinized each wedding guest, Isaac was obliged to shake Cowboy's fist. "Luck," Isaac said, smiling into the ruffles of a sleeve. Cowboy welcomed Isaac with the scorn and panoply of a master pimp. He wore a midnight-blue ensemble, with a silk cravat, a cummerbund, and trousers wider than a skirt; his rank, "Chief of Detectives," was filigreed on cufflinks made of speckled pearl. Cowboy had dropped thirteen thousand dollars to capture a hall big enough to launch his balding daughter, and he'd hang himself with the magnificent drapes in the PC's office (installed by Teddy Roosevelt seventy years ago), before he allowed Isaac to muck up his one day of glory. He'd made certain that Isaac and his boyfriend were exiled to a table practically inside the kitchen, so that the reek of chicken fat could remind them of their low station. Blue Eyes disgusted him even more than Isaac did. It was pretty boys like Coen who had toyed with Barney's girl, disappointing Anita again and again until Cowboy had to act. He produced a bridegroom for Anita, a fifty-eight-year-old merchant without any merchandise, a bachelor with incredible dental bills, an orphan hungry for a father-in-law who could bully detectives in all five boroughs. Barney found a niche for him on Schermerhorn Street, a crack in the wall two pushcarts deep, and turned this orphan into a haberdasher. The Chief of Detectives couldn't have his oldest daughter in bed with a propertyless man.

"Isaac, you shouldn't worry. Stanley Chin won't die of hospital food. My men have been feeding him chocolate bars."

Cowboy deserved to gloat; he'd secured Anita for life (the haberdasher would have had to orphan his skull if he disappeared from Schermerhorn Street), he'd grabbed a lollipop away from Isaac in Corona, and he'd already whispered to the PC how Blue Eyes had been caught with cunty Marilyn. But

Isaac stepped around him, muttering awkward hellos to the PC and his wife, and steered south along the wedding table until he reached the First Dep. Isaac hadn't come to discuss police business with his boss. He didn't tell O'Roarke about the nest of car thieves his "angels" had uncovered in the Third Division, cops supplying North Jersey gamblers with Fords and Buicks. Isaac had the details in his head; he would only burden O'Roarke after he was ready to pounce on the cops and rip their nest apart. Isaac leaned into the side of the table. "Can I get you and Mrs. O'Roarke something from the buffet, Commissioner Ned?"

The First Dep watched Isaac with crisp green eyes that could withstand the corrosion of drugs, and the radium he had to swallow; before the tumor in his throat began to eat away areas of his concentration, O'Roarke had been the most feared cop in New York. The Police Commissioner was strictly the Mayor's bride; enmeshed in city politics, a PC would vanish within a few seasons. The First Dep had remained in office thirty years. He broke in each new Commissioner, and had to sweep up the junk of the old PC. O'Roarke was the nearest thing to permanence a cop would ever know. And now the Deputy Commissioner was dying in his chair.

Gentle with Isaac, the First Dep asked for Coen. "Why is Manfred so far away? Is he catching fly balls? I can't see him from this end of the table."

"It's nothing, Commissioner Ned. Cowboy doesn't want him near the bride."

"That's fine for Cowboy. What about us? I always cheat on my indigestion when Manfred smiles."

"I can bring him, but he'll get into trouble down here. He's much better off in Cowboy's woods."

Isaac sent for Blue Eyes. Coen passed the tables reserved for detective sergeants, minor relatives, and lowly precinct captains who sneered at the angel boy behind their napkins because they couldn't afford to alienate Isaac in the open. Isaac disappeared. He'd suffered through the smorgasbord, showing his eyeteeth to commissioners, deputy mayors, and choice Rosenblatts, and he crept out of the hall on ripple soles to avoid a sit-down dinner, where he would have had to swallow turkey breasts, string beans, Neptune cabbage, and shreds of fruit cocktail with Barney's "crows" and a hierarchy of fat cops. Blue Eyes could double for him. Isaac tapped Coen's chin on his way out. "Watch the First Dep. If he spits blood, or anything, you call me."

Coen had to shift for himself. He couldn't abscond, like his Chief. He was resigned to a dead Sunday. The First Dep found a chair for him. Blue Eyes was squeezed into the wedding table. Cowboy gobbled grapefruit sections with dark spit on his tongue. He couldn't overrule Commissioner Ned. Coen would have to stay. The smorgasbord was wheeled out, pushing towards the kitchen like an exhausted mountain, delicacies tottering in their trays. A three-piece band appeared during the first course, a saxophone, an accordion, and a bass fiddle. The band set itself up in what had earlier been the inner ring of the smorgasbord. Wedding guests were encouraged to dance between courses, so the kitchen crew would have the chance to clear every table; the assistant chefs had to decorate five hundred platters with minced potato balls for the second course.

The hard scream of the saxophone cluttered the hall with a whiff of metal. The fiddler had thickened fingers. The accordionist could barely tease a cop out onto the floor. With pistols stuck in their belts, most cops were reluctant to dance. Their wives didn't brood over this; they wanted to dance with Coen. Blue Eyes had to leave the table. The "crows" were giving him murderous looks. One by one the wives embraced him. The accordionist had prepared a spicy Hebrew song for the Hands of Esau and Irish jigs for the Holy Rood of Catholic cops. The wives interrupted his melodies. They demanded something slow. Coen went from fox-trot to fox-trot. He couldn't tire the wives. They forced him to change partners in the middle of a dip. The constant scrub of skin gave Coen an unfortunate erection. The wives seized upon such vulnerabilities to dance up close to Blue Eyes. The husbands grew exceedingly grim. They were taking mental target practice at the Neptune Manor, popping Coen's pretty ears and pretty mouth. Blue Eyes was intolerable to them. These men trudged through their tours of duty worrying about the spies the First Deputy had planted in their stationhouses; they didn't have to see Isaac's angel bumping with their wives.

The haberdasher's bride must have sensed Coen's desperation. She got up, holding pieces of gown with a fist, to cut in on the wives and lure them away from Coen. But she hadn't reckoned on the delicacy of Coen's lines, the touch of a fingernail in her palm, the feel of an embarrassed prick. Her face began to erupt, blotches glowing under her veil. She sucked her own spit to distract herself. The haberdasher was mortified. His Anita danced two feet from him with her wrists unfurled. The creases in her back were unmistakable. Anita was bending to Coen. The haberdasher sought his father-in-law with narrowed cheeks. Cowboy didn't idle at the wedding table; he'd been plotting Coen's downfall from the beginning of the fox-trot. Barney knew a grocer in Bath Beach, a kind

Italian boy, who might be willing to shut Coen's eyes for a hundred dollars. The grocer came with a guarantee; he wouldn't accept a penny if he should happen to fail.

But the wedding hall was brushed by a miracle; Coen's prick went down. Anita bent away from him. She kept a few inches between Blue Eyes and herself. Her fierce complexion dwindled under the veil. Soon she could have her native coloring again. Coen escorted her to the table, the commissioners clapping feebly for the bride. The haberdasher was having evil thoughts about his wedding night. Blue Eyes sat with his nose in the silverware, determined not to peek at Anita's veil. Barney could politick with wedding guests now that sweetheart Coen had his dancing shoes under the table. The waiters were coming; little feathers of steam rose off the turkey breasts, which had their own potato balls and a gulley of peas.

Isaac enjoyed Sunday afternoons at Centre Street when the commissioner's rooms weren't swollen with detectives and boyish cops who served as runners and secretaries. He could poke through half-deserted halls without confronting dignitaries, or FBI men, and visiting inspectors from the London murder squad and the French Sûreté; just Sunday cops, like Isaac himself, who were married to their notebooks and their shields, and who loved the smell of dark woodwork, and the comforts of a sinking building: Headquarters was falling into the ground at the rate of two inches every five years. Stanchions had been put around the building to shore it up, and the city engineers claimed they could retard the sinkage by almost an inch.

Isaac ducked under the stanchions, which clung to Headquarters like an enormous iron skirt, passed through a tight front door (Headquarters had to screen its enemies and its friends), and paused at the security booth; the guard, who worked in Brooklyn the rest of the week, sat behind a bulletproof cage. This Sunday man had a shrewdness for picking girls off the street. He would babble to them as they stood outside the cage, their tits against the green bulletproof glass. Phinney, the Sunday man, was too discreet to invite them into the booth. There was a girl with him now. Issac could only see one side of her face. Her legs were bare under her pea coat. The stretch of her calves appealed to Isaac, but he couldn't understand how any girl could go without socks in the middle of February. He saluted the guard. Phinney said, "Good afternoon, Chief," with a cowlike smile. Isaac could afford to be lax with him. The Irish Mafia would rush to communion after Barney's wedding: Headquarters was free of commissioners.

Isaac went upstairs. The duty sergeant who belonged to Commissioner O'Roarke was sleeping on a bench. Isaac wouldn't disturb him. He closed his office door with a soft pull of the knob. He was going to play back several tapes a stoolie of his had prepared of cops shaking down a supermarket. He sat behind his desk searching for spools. He stabbed his fingers in a drawer, but Isaac wouldn't howl out his pain. He could swear his desk had begun to shiver. A loud crump, like the pop of paper bags in his skull, catapulted Isaac off his chair. The window was shitting glass. Isaac had his cheek in the wall. Shock waves came up through the floor, thick patterns of congested air that shoved smoke into Isaac's mouth. He crawled out of the room, spitting up phlegm and crumbled plaster. Splits had developed in the ceiling. The walls had turned to bark.

The duty sergeant was under his bench. His head emerged to glower at Isaac, whose scalp was mostly white (the Chief hadn't shaken off the plaster). "Mercy, Isaac, it's happened. The building's caved in. Will they get to us, Chief? Will they be able to tunnel us out?"

The sergeant's delirium made Isaac smile. "Relax, Malone. It will be an easy rescue. We couldn't have sunk more than a thousand feet." The sergeant drew his head all the way in. Isaac felt ashamed. "Malone? I'm sorry . . . it was a small bomb. It must have gone off in the bathroom under my office."

Malone didn't move his head. "Isaac, could it be those crazy Puerto Ricans, or the Black Liberation boys? Were they trying to bury a few cops alive?"

"No, no, that kiss was meant for me."

Isaac ran down to the next floor. He walked into the bathroom with a handkerchief over his face. A pea coat had been dropped under the sink. Isaac called himself a dummy and a toad; he should have stared harder at that girl without her stockings. Phinney couldn't have brought her into Headquarters. The girl was using him. He had a better view of her face. It was bitten with glass and burnt powder. He couldn't find her underwear. She'd come to Isaac in a pea coat, moccasins, and skin. Three cracked mayonnaise jars were near the body. It took Isaac time to sniff the jars before he noticed that one of the girl's arms had been ripped off in the blast.

Two men charged into the bathroom wearing helmets, hard aprons, asbestos jump suits, and gigantic terry cloth gloves. They were members of the bomb squad stationed at the Police Academy. Isaac stepped in front of them. "You can go home," he said. "The case is closed. You'll hear about it in my report."

Both helmets muttered "Fuck you" at Isaac. This was their turf. No one could tell them they were intruders at a bombing. They had to sift through the debris.

Isaac mentioned his name and then shouted into the asbestos hats. "I have the First Dep's warranty. If you touch a piece of glass, if you disturb anything, I'll have your tongues burned."

The men shrugged behind their aprons. They couldn't wrestle Isaac the Pure with terry cloth gloves. They peeked at the dead girl's crotch and walked out, uninterested in a dismembered arm. Phinney, the Sunday man, was crouching by the stairs, his face gone sallow. He called into the bathroom, frightened to step inside. "Isaac, who is that stupid girl?"

"A lollipop, Esther Rose."

"She said she had to go pee . . . I didn't . . . Isaac, how should I know she was smuggling hot ones under her coat?"

"Phinney, you fucked yourself. Headquarters isn't a public piss pot. Nobody's supposed to get up those stairs. They'll wire you to the ceiling and bleed your pension out of your ears."

Phinney chewed on a knuckle. "What should I tell them, Isaac? Gimme a story, please."

"It takes a clever man to lie, Phinney. You tell the truth. Now shut up and get back to your post. Cowboy's only a river away. There'll be a hundred cops on our heads any minute."

10.

M<small>ARILYN</small> had difficulties sustaining her new bachelorhood. There was more than one woman in her father's house. Isaac had brought his "fiancée" to Rivington Street. He couldn't have Ida Stutz prowling in her own flat when Rupert Weil could attack a fire escape. So the three of them had to blow air in two small rooms. The girls couldn't get along. Marilyn tried. But Ida was fidgety around an educated girl. She grew ashamed of her sweat, and the bits of cheese that always fell into her hair while she was making blintzes at the restaurant. Her body seemed like a miserable article next to Marilyn's fine elbows and goyisher ribs. Ida sniffled into the cheese; she wanted to throw her head in a tub of barley soup and drown.

Marilyn could only relax after Isaac and his "fiancée" went to work. Then she had Rivington Street to herself. She would bathe in the afternoon, scratch her fingernails, consider the veins in her hand. She missed Blue Eyes. But if she connived behind her father's back and rushed uptown to Coen, she'd ruin his chances with Isaac and the First Dep. Marilyn sensed her father's vindictiveness. Isaac was jealous of Coen.

As Isaac's bachelor daughter, she shared the toilet with an old man across the hall. This old man hogged the facilities. A bachelor himself, he despised any woman who peed sitting down. Marilyn had to flush the toilet after him; he was much too squeamish to touch the plunger attached to the water box. She might have avoided the bachelor altogether if he had bothered to close the toilet door. He would sit with his pants bunched around a nail over his head, bang his raw knees with a fist, and sing outrageous songs through the door, courtship songs, Marilyn imagined, because of the bachelor's feverish intonation. She had no other clue. The songs wouldn't cohere into a language Marilyn understood; he seemed to chirp scraps of English, Yiddish, and Hungarian. Marilyn had little desire to tease out their intent.

This morning, desperate to pee, she stumbled into the toilet. She swerved to miss colliding with the bachelor's knees. Her bosoms struck the wall. "Christ," she said. He sat clicking his teeth, with an incredible red prick that rose out of his belly to serenade an Irish-Jewish girl. Marilyn wanted Coen.

❖

Not even the PC could get Isaac away from his desk. His subordinates were baffled by Isaac's foul mood. A lollipop who sabotaged herself couldn't hurt im. saac was a hero.

Hadn't he survived Esther's homemade bombs, concoctions in mayonnaise jars? What did the Chief have to mourn?

Isaac sat for hours without a sign of slackness in his heavy cheeks. He wouldn't humor his men. They were part of the rubber-gun squad, former "angels" of Isaac's who had suffered the ultimate humiliation: they had their .45s snatched from them by the PC because of overzealousness in the street. The medical bureau accused them of being trigger crazy. They'd shot off too many noses, it seems. Now they clerked for Isaac. They were sensitive to each little shift in Isaac's character, to his porcupine scalp, those rigid patches behind his ears that betrayed his anxiousness. What could the Chief be waiting for?

The phone rang around three in the afternoon. The rubber-gun squad watched Isaac's scalp unbridle; these men had grown psychic about the noises a telephone could make. Isaac put his tongue near the mouthpiece. "Hello?"

"Is this Isaac the Pure?"

The air blew out of Isaac's cheeks, leaving them soft.

"I'm calling about Esther Rose. You killed her, you pimp. She brought you soup, and you had to throw her on top of a shithill."

"Some soup," Isaac said. "It came in a funny jar. Rupert, where are you?"

"Wouldn't you like to know? Isaac, did she cry when you tortured her? Or did she spit in your policeman's face?"

"Rupert, we have to talk. I'll meet you anywhere you say."

The rubber-gun boys were scrambling to monitor Rupert's call. The Chief warned them away from the sound equipment with a wag of his jaw. They couldn't believe Isaac would cow to a lollipop.

"Was it the pretty blond detective who took care of Esther's arm? I'll fix him too."

"Blue Eyes? He never saw Esther Rose. Rupert, stay off the street. Some grim Italian boys are looking for you."

"Isaac, you trying to hold me while your technicians trace me to a telephone booth? Forget about it. I'm signing off."

"You're overrating us, Rupert. The FBI untangles wires, not us. We're primitive men."

"You'll be primitive sooner than you think. I'll play with your jawbone. I'll soak your teeth in pickled water. I'll send your guts to Headquarters, C.O.D. You'll be remembered, Isaac. You'll wish to God you hadn't fucked with Esther. Goodbye."

Isaac held a cold telephone in his lap. The rubber-gun squad shied away from him. The Chief was in the middle of a brainstorm. The medical examiner and the fingerprint boys who dusted the mayonnaise jars had given him nothing beyond the fact of Esther's immolation. Isaac had to scratch with his thumbs. Careless girls don't leave their coats under a sink. Esther's nakedness cut into the easy theory of an accidental death. Did she love to finger bombs without her clothes? Who'd believe a girl would want to die with Isaac? He hoped Rupert would reveal Esther to him. The boy's instructions were slow. Rupert turned Isaac into a murderer.

He'd sent Coen deep into Brooklyn to interview Esther's family. Coen barely got out alive. The Spagnuolos cursed him and attacked him with their fingernails. They disclaimed any knowledge of Esther. Isaac wasn't satisfied. He'd dealt with stranger Jews than these. Hadn't he made the tzaddik of Williamsburg smile? He'd danced with Hasidim in a syna-

gogue that was bigger than a soccer field. So Isaac went
searching for Esther. He took Brodsky along. Isaac wouldn't
have sought company in Manhattan or the Bronx, where he
could determine any street with his nose. But Brooklyn was
a second Arabia, uncrossable for Isaac without a limousine,
a desert of contradicting neighborhoods, murderous, soft,
with pockets of air that could drive chills through a cop's
sturdy drawers. Isaac found Esther's people in a block of
private houses near Gravesend and Coney Island Creek. He
wasn't invited inside. A man in a skullcap who could have
been Esther's father, uncle, or older brother (his twitching
eyebrows and pendulous ears made his age impossible to tell)
came out to greet Isaac with a butcher knife. Isaac backed off
the sidewalk, disenchanted with Sephardic Jews. He signaled
to Brodsky, wiggling at Manhattan with a fist.

Now he was calling for Brodsky again. Isaac wanted the
morgue at Bellevue. The rubber-gun squad crammed his
raincoat with a fresh supply of pencils (the Chief liked to
scribble on his rides with Brodsky). The chauffeur had a
glum look. He preferred to keep away from hospitals and
morgues. Isaac wasn't trying to push Brodsky towards a
ghoulish medical examiner. The Chief was after Esther's
body. The Spagnuolos had left her in a city icebox, unclaimed.
If the Hands of Esau refused to bury a Jewish lollipop on
society grounds (Barney Rosenblatt had the power to stall
Isaac's request), he would fish for a grave out of his own
pocket, a grave with a legitimate marker.

The morgue attendant was coy with Isaac. He swore on his
life that Esther had disappeared. "Isaac, you have the authority. Tear down the walls. The coroner's afraid of the

First Dep. But you won't find shit. The girl was picked up."

"Did they row her out to Ward's Island on the paupers' run?"

The thought of Esther being dumped in a potter's field maddened Isaac. It was gruesome to him. A grave would be turned out every ten or twenty years to accommodate a different crop of bones.

The attendant smiled. "Isaac, it wasn't Ward's Island. Somebody signed for her."

"Show me the release, you scumbag."

The attendant returned with a long card.

"Was it a relative?" Isaac muttered.

"No, it says 'admirer.' "

"What's the admirer's name? . . . could it be Rupert?"

The attendant squinted at the card. "Isaac, it aint so clear. One word. It begins with a Z."

"Zorro," Brodsky said, with sudden illumination, his chin in the attendant's shoulder.

The attendant curled his eyes. "Isaac, you can't trick the morgue. Who's Zorro?"

"One of the Guzmann boys." The cemetery was in Bronx-ville, where the Guzmanns had a family plot. Checking with another attendant, Isaac discovered that Zorro Guzmann had snatched Esther's body only two hours ago. He rushed out of the morgue.

Brodsky fumbled behind the Chief. "Isaac, it makes no sense. What could the Guzmanns do with a lollipop? Are they planning to revive her? Will they sell her in the street?"

A tribe of Marranos from Peru, pickpockets, thieves, and pimps, the Guzmanns had settled in the Bronx, becoming the policy bankers of Boston Road; they thrived amid Latinos, poor Irishers, blacks, and ancient Jews. Isaac hadn't concerned himself with their penny plays. But the tribe was beginning to infest Manhattan. The Guzmanns would kidnap young girls from the Port Authority and auction them to local whorehouses. Isaac meant to squeeze the tribe out of his borough. The lollipops were slowing him down. He could no longer concentrate on grubby pimps.

The chauffeur took him to Bronxville. The Guzmann burial ground was a hummock of frozen grass. Three old men stood shivering over a fresh scar in the hummock. They were expert mourners. The Guzmanns had hired them to wail for Esther. They wore the caftans of a chief rabbi, only each of them came with a pectoral cross. Zorro was with them, in a checkered overcoat. Brodsky nudged the Chief with a loud cackle. "Isaac, should I throw him down the hill? Let these old men mourn for Zorro while they're here. One tap on the head, and you can close the Guzmann case. Zorro won't have a brain left."

Isaac pointed to a man on the other side of the hummock, a man without Zorro's penchant for clothes; he had earmuffs from a Bronx variety store, a scarf as mottled as a hankie, a thickness of sweaters, overalls that ballooned in the seat and stopped just below the calf, galoshes that wouldn't buckle. His nostrils were flat, and he had a forehead that was uncommonly wide.

"Do me a favor, Brodsky. Whisper your threats from now on. That's Jorge over there. Zorro's big brother. Bullets can't touch him. He has elephant skin. He'll shovel dirt in our eyes if we move on Zorro. So be nice."

Isaac walked up to Zorro Guzmann (César was his baptismal name) without a hand in his pocket, so Jorge wouldn't misinterpret Isaac's peaceful signs and come galloping down the hummock with squeaky galoshes and his earmuffs askew. Zorro had mud on his pigskin shoes. His coat of many colors turned orange in the afternoon. Isaac tried not to stare at Zorro's dainty feet.

"Zorro, since when does Papa interest himself in the affairs of a Yeshiva girl? Brooklyn isn't your borough."

"Isaac, you calling my father illiterate? He reads the *Daily News*. The girl's a Ladina, isn't she? You think my father's going to allow her to sleep in an unholy grave? Not when she's a Spanish Jew. You see those criers on the hill? The holy men. They've been cursing Esther's mother and father since two o'clock."

"That's a touching story, but are you sure Papa isn't sanctifying Esther because she tried to murder me?"

"Isaac, don't blaspheme in a graveyard. My father's a religious man. He doesn't care if you live or die."

"Good for him. Zorro, I respect your family. I never interfered with Guzmann business on Boston Road. So take the wax out of your ear. Manhattan's not for you. The cockroaches have a nasty sting."

"Isaac, I can't even spell Manhattan. Why would I go there to live?"

Isaac was finished with obligatory advice. He had plans to shred Zorro's spectacular coat. He would push the Guzmanns into a sewer once he caught those fish in Manhattan.

"César, aren't you going to ask me about Blue Eyes?"

Zorro dug the earth with the pigskin on his feet. "Don't say blue. Blue is a filthy color in my religion. Isaac, teach yourself some history. All the magistrates used to wear blue cloaks in Portugal and Spain six hundred years ago. Can't you figure? A dark color could prevent the stink of a Jew from poisoning their armpits."

"Did your father tell you that?"

"No, I learnt it from my brothers."

Zorro's four brothers, Alejandro, Topal, Jorge, and Jerónimo, were Bronx wisemen who couldn't read the letters off a street sign, or manage the intricacies of a revolving door. Jerónimo, the oldest, slept in a crib.

"César, you still haven't asked me about Coen?"

"There's nothing to ask. Manfred flew from Papa's candy store. He made his nest with you."

Coen had been raised on Boston Road, where Papa Guzmann maintained his empire under the cover of egg creams and soft candy. It was Papa who shoved Coen's parents towards suicide, controlling them with little gifts of money until the miserable egg store they had came into Papa's hands.

Zorro edged away from Isaac. He was in Bronxville at his father's bidding, to put an unwanted Ladina under frozen grass, with three Christian rabbis in attendance, hovering over the Guzmanns' sacred mound. "Isaac, this is a funeral. I can't talk no more."

Isaac trudged with Brodsky down from the cemetery. The chauffeur spied at Jorge Guzmann from the corner of his sleeve; he was baffled that a moron with open galoshes could frighten the Chief.

"Please, Isaac, lemme pop this Jorge once behind the ear. We'll see what flows out, water, piss, or blood."

The Chief closed Brodsky's face with a horrible scowl. He

wasn't looking for company. He sat at the back of the car. He could have taken off Brodsky's lip with the heat spilling from both his eyes. "Esther," he muttered. He was sick of a world of lollipops.

11.

A GIRL could go crazy smelling pot cheese in her father's refrigerator. Stuck between Isaac and his "fiancée," Marilyn fell to brooding over the conditions of her past and present life: Sarah Lawrence, three husbands, pot cheese, and Rivington Street in seven years. She had to get free of blintzes and Ida Stutz. Marilyn needed Blue Eyes, but her father had stolen him away. She put on her winter coat, locked Isaac's door, and went into the street. There was no escaping Isaac. They nodded to her at the matzoh factory, at the appetizing store with prunes in the window, at the Hungarian bakery with its crusts of dark bread that could cure widows and divorcées of constipation, boils, or the gout.

"Hello, Miss Sidel. Tell me, how's the Chief today? Honey, don't be bashful. Take a piece of strudel for your father and yourself. Please. Why shove a pocketbook in my face? It's too early in the morning to cash a ten-dollar bill."

The whole fucking East Side was her father's house. She had to shop in Little Italy if she wanted to stay alive. In her father's territories no one would allow her to pay for her goods. A block from Rivington Street she was loaded down with packages. She had strudel, whole wheat matzohs, salt sticks, and pumpkin seeds. She walked to Bummy's on East Broadway, where she could get some relief from Isaac's worshipers. At Bummy's her father was despised.

Marilyn ordered a whiskey sour with two stabs of lemon and a lick of salt. She knew about the old crook that worked in Bummy's kitchen, one-eyed Gulavitch, maimed by her father. Isaac had poked his knuckles in Gula's eye. She wondered if the old crook might revenge himself on her. But she couldn't see into the kitchen.

Bummy Gilman came over to her stool. He was perturbed about having a skinny girl with tits in his bar. A cunt like Marilyn could bring trouble to him. Isaac was capable of wrecking any bar.

"Bummy, don't frown," she said. "I'm not Isaac's messenger. I didn't come with greetings from him."

"Marilyn, who's calling you a stoolpigeon? Not me." He shouted to the barman. "George, this lady needs more ice in her glass."

The barman arrived with a cylinder of ice. Then he withdrew to his station, fingering the buttons on his red jacket. Bummy left Marilyn to whisper in the barman's ear. "George, keep her busy. If she asks for apple pie, give it to her."

The barman licked his teeth. "God, would I love to get into that."

"Forget it, George. She's poison. Her father has terrific

hands. He could pull your nose off with half a finger. She's a dragon lady. I wouldn't lie."

Bummy strolled into his kitchen, searching for Gula One Eye. Gula was crouching over the potato bin. He could flick warts off a potato faster than a Marrano pickpocket from the Bronx could reach inside your pants. "Gula," Bummy said with a cackle. "Would you like to get laid?"

"Bummy, you shouldn't joke," Gulavitch said, climbing off the bin.

"Sweetheart, you know who's sitting out there with her legs crossed? Isaac's daughter. She's itching for you."

"Let her itch."

"At least make her a present. You lost an eye. Get it back from her."

"That's no good," Gulavitch said. "What's she done? I'll pay Isaac, not the girl."

Bummy couldn't argue with a feeble-minded crook. He returned to George. His head was boiling with images of Isaac. The Chief owned East Broadway. Bummy had to dance with the big Jewish bear at Headquarters, curtsy to Isaac, or move his bar to Brooklyn. He was sick of it. "George, you got the green light. The dragon lady's all yours. Take her. I don't care. But watch yourself. She bruises. If Isaac ever catches your thumb marks on her skin, you're a dead man."

George stroked one of his red cuffs. "Bummy, leave it to me."

Bummy sat down near his register, fingering yesterday's receipts, as he watched the barman sweet-talk Marilyn the Wild. He had to marvel at George's abilities. The barman waltzed with his thumbs on Marilyn's ass before Bummy could finish the receipts. There was a little arena behind the bar where Bummy staged dog fights for special customers, or an occasional burlesque show (the girls who took off their clothes at Bummy's place were borrowed from Zorro Guzmann). The arena became a dance floor whenever Bummy was short of bulldogs and Zorro's girls.

Marilyn went into the arena with George. She couldn't get by on whiskey sours and salt under her lip. She needed some sweat and male companionship to ease her off Rivington Street and the color of Coen's eyes. She wasn't solemn about a cock in the furls of her groin. She knew what it meant to dance with George. She didn't intercept the track of his wrist. George liked to cuddle with a finger in her underpants, and Sinatra on Bummy's phonograph machine. "Baby," he said, "come home with me."

Silences couldn't discourage him. George was a patient barman. He ran for Bummy's keys. "Bummy, it's open house. I can tell." His hands were trembling. "I swear, she's three yards wide."

Bummy gave him the keys to the bedroom he maintained over the bar. It was a retreat for his customers, who could romance one of Zorro's burlesque queens without having to abandon East Broadway. George led Marilyn through the kitchen, where she could peek at Gula and his potato bin (the bin had deep sides, and was very, very dark), and marched her up Bummy's private staircase. He undressed her, with the keys in the door, piling her skirt and blouse on a chair. He was much more fastidious about his own red jacket, which he refused to stick on a hanger in Bummy's closet until both shoulders were aligned. He wore garters around his

knees, and a truss to keep his hernia in place. George had no
pubic hair. Marilyn saw a lump, shaped like a pea, at the
top of George's thigh, when the truss came off. He kissed her
with his garters on. His plucked crotch had an itchy feel. He
pushed her down into Bummy's queen-sized bed, the hernia
traveling along the wedges in his thigh.

Marilyn wasn't spooked by a pea sliding under some skin.
A man with a hernia might have made her into a passionate
girl, only George was too gruff. He climbed on Marilyn, with
his garters scratching her legs, and forced his way in. She
didn't complain. She hadn't come to Bummy's for a tea
party. She had whiskey in her lungs. She endured the rub of
garters, and George's mean little plunges. She couldn't even
hold him by the ears to catch a piece of his rhythm. He
wouldn't lower his head. His orgasm was like a snarl. He
climbed off Marilyn, hitched up the belts of his truss, and
brought his jacket out of the closet. "I'm in a rush," he said.
"Bummy needs me . . . he gets lonely when I'm away from
the bar."

Marilyn stayed in bed. She didn't want to creep downstairs too soon and suck on a maraschino cherry. Whiskey
sours would turn her against Coen. She fought her bitterness
by grabbing Bummy's lavender sheets. Jesus, Joseph, and
Mary, if Blue Eyes wouldn't come inside her, she could always
look for George.

She got dressed finally, retrieving her stuff from the chair.
She couldn't find a washcloth in Bummy's room, so she
walked out with milk on her thigh. "Being a spinster isn't so
bad. I'll survive without Manfred Coen." She wasn't nervous
about the kitchen. Gulavitch could have her neck to play

with. She'd help him drive his thumbs into her windpipe. Gula called her over to the bin. "Missy, I got a potato face for you."

He'd carved a warty potato with his nails. The face had nostrils, ears, lips, and a pair of warts for eyes. Gula made a sloping chin, and the depressions of a widow's peak, giving the potato the twisted features of a penitent. Marilyn wasn't put off by somber details. The potato was a kindness to her. She had a fit of blubbering, ravaged by the markings on a lopsided face. The gift had an urgency no husband could bring. Gula must have seen the mad streak in her when she crossed the kitchen with George. Was he telling her with the potato, Missy, you aint alone? She could have screamed, "Blue balls and father shit," into Gula's chest without feeling ashamed. He drew a rag out of his sleeve for Marilyn. She wiped her eyes with it.

"Don't sit at the bar. Bummy's a cocksucker. Nobody loves you here. Tell your father Gula One Eye fucks him in the nose."

"I will, Mr. Gulavitch. I promise."

And she sailed out of the kitchen with the rag in her fist, passing Bummy, who mocked the ratty glide of her skirt, and George, who cursed her for inflaming the lump in his groin. Marilyn didn't care. She grabbed her packages off the stool, the matzohs and the pumpkin seeds, and left East Broadway.

12.

─────────────

Rupert clawed Esther's furniture and artifacts, a broken chair, a pincushion used by Spagnuolo seamstresses, ribbons from her Yeshiva days, tampons in a candy box, pieces of colored chalk, assorted chemicals, and a crusted pot, all the worldly goods she had brought with her to the tenement on Suffolk Street, Esther's last address. Rupert was hungry to curse her. His fingers mauled the pincushion. The ribbons disintegrated after a few pulls. The chalk bled green and yellow against his palms. He couldn't say the word "bitch."

Why had he been so dumb about the ingredients in Esther's pot? She must have stolen a recipe from *The Anarchist Cookbook*. Stinky Rupert forgot how to smell a bomb. Did Esther invent a woolly fuse? Ignite her jars with Tampax? Or did Isaac nab her at the door, bite her tits, throw her in a room, and supply the match? Such sequences weren't Rupert's concern. However Esther died, he would pinch Isaac soon as he could.

It was the Chinese New Year, the Year of the Swan, and Rupert had a prior commitment. He intended to free Stanley Chin. With Esther thick in his skull, a hard, bitter longing that nudged him with mad ideas (was it kosher to fuck a dead girl?), shaking him with impressions of her, mind and body, that could unhinge him any minute, he planned his attack on St. Bartholomew's. He would tear out the throats of detectives and nurses who got in his way. He would take the prisoner on a piggyback ride, ferry him to Chinatown (Rupert could wink across a river), so Stanley could celebrate the New Year in a Chinese café.

Rupert first met him at Seward Park, where they were freshmen together. Stanley was a muscle boy, a bill collector for Chinese merchants and landlords, and a bodyguard belonging to the Pell Street Republican Club. It was the futility of Republicans in Chinatown that impressed Rupert: Stanley Chin always picked the losing side. He was a boy from Hong Kong, in love with barbells, American cigarettes, and Bruce Lee. He could crumble bricks with his teeth, kick through a wall, smash the legs of a table, until the Snapping Dragons of Pell Street, Stanley's old gang, sent him to St. Bartholomew's with crippled fingers and toes. Rupert felt responsible; he had drawn Stanley out of Chinatown, recruited him to his own brittle cause, the dismantling of Isaac, and introduced him to Esther Rose.

Gorillas from Mulberry Street were cruising Rupert's neighborhood with firm instructions in their heads. Amerigo Genussa of the Garibaldi social club had warned them not to return to Little Italy without some token off the body of

Rupert Weil; an ear, a fingernail, a Jewish bellybutton, anything that would leave him incapacitated for the next ten
years. Rupert could see them in their long gray coats, huddling on Suffolk Street while they blew between their knuckles to soften a chill that was murderously close. A rotten wind
off the Bowery must have pushed them onto Rupert's heels.
He had no respect for gorillas. The idea of bullying for profit
was loathsome to him. He would have hurled Esther's chair
off the fire escape, watched it float down on top of their
brains, if he hadn't been in such a rush.

He climbed out of a cellar window at the back of the
house. The gorillas could blow air for the rest of their lives;
the snot would have to freeze in their noses before they could
find Rupert Weil. He ran to the pickle factory on Broome.
The merchants had lit a small fire on the premises to keep
their pickles warm. The brine coming off the barrels stuck to
Rupert's heart. He would have liked to soak his ears in a
barrel. A fat man snorted at him with obvious disgruntle-
ment. It was Tony Brill. The journalist had been waiting near
the pickles for an hour.

"Gimme," Rupert said.

"First talk. What did it feel like beating on Isaac's
mother?"

Rupert glowered at the journalist. "It didn't feel. We had
to smoke out Isaac. That was the necessary thing."

"Did you enjoy it?"

"You a creep?" Rupert said.

"But you almost killed her."

"Na. She fell. She hit her head. That wasn't us . . . listen,
it's not so hard to kill when you got Isaac for a teacher."

The journalist removed a collection of dollar bills from

his pocket, twenty singles that he'd borrowed from his landlady and his current employer, an underground newspaper called *The Toad*. "Now tell me your story," he said, his tongue twisting in his mouth. "All of it. You, Esther, and Stanley Chin."

Rupert said, "Tomorrow."

Spit leaked off the journalist's face. "Are you crazy? Are you insane? It could snow tomorrow. I could die of the flu. Money talks. I'll take the story, or the twenty bills go back to me."

Rupert was halfway to Ludlow Street. "You'll get it," he shouted, the dollars squeezed inside his fist.

The journalist was trying to keep up with him. "Rupert, do you ever dream about Isaac's mother?"

"Only when my stomach is empty."

"How often is that?"

"Every other night."

❖

Stanley Chin couldn't have lunch or dinner without two detectives at his side. These gentlemen ate his stewed prunes. Stanley ignored the nurses' harping about the state of his bowels. He was their favorite prisoner; the nurses of St. Bartholomew's could adore a delinquent with a beautiful face. But his bowels shrank after detectives Murray and John told him Sunday's news: the Jew girl, Esther Rose, had eaten powerful mayonnaise at Headquarters; the medical examiners had tweezed her eyebrows off the wall. The detectives poked behind their ears. They worked for Big Jew Rosenblatt, but they wouldn't cry for Esther Rose. They'd handcuff this China boy to the bed if they had to. They were expecting Blue Eyes. Isaac had to send his "angels" down to kidnap Stanley Chin. The Chief was losing face.

Stanley was beholden to detectives Murray and John; he couldn't reach very far with fingers stuck in plaster mittens. So Murray, John, or a nurse had to put the water glass against his lip, change his pajamas, turn the radio on and off, take itchy mattress hairs off his leg. The detectives noticed Stanley was in a rotten mood. He hadn't asked them to scratch his back once during their last three shifts. His biceps were growing haggard. The ropes of muscle in his neck had gone to sleep. He had Esther in his guts.

It was no puppy love, the passion of a Hong Kong boy for a girl with white skin, an Anglo from Brooklyn, an ordinary "round eyes." It had nothing to do with pale colors. Esther was darker than him. She had sweat in her armpits, a generous damp run from her shoulders to her elbows that made Stanley sneeze a lot. She couldn't have enticed him with her frizzy hair. And it wasn't her religious training (he'd never heard of Yeshivas before Esther Rose). It was a clutter of things; the throaty rasp of her voice, the way she rolled her sleeves, her ability to argue ancient and medieval philosophies (Esther knew the lore of five or six Arab priests), the grab of her nipples under her one dark shirt, the shape of her toes, the sores she had on her arms and knees from painting ceilings with chalk, the chalkings themselves, lashes of color that exemplified bitter mouths, long tongues, and hard, swol-

len genitals that grew and twitched without relief. The horrors
Esther manufactured on a ceiling or a wall comforted Stanley; they were shriekings he felt inside his own head.

He'd been dreaming of Esther with a pill the nurses had
stuck in his mouth, a yellow thing that he would soon squash
under his tongue, when he saw a wizard come into the room,
a wizard with bony ears, in a St. Bartholomew orderly's coat
a size too small, pushing a wheelchair with his sleeves. The
wizard steered around the detectives' triple-tone shoes. "Pardon me," he said. Detective Murray didn't care for the
orderly's tight cheeks, but he wouldn't contradict hospital
rules.

The wizard smiled. "Therapy room. Help me get him off
the mattress."

Detective John raised the slats of Stanley's hospital bed,
and the two detectives sat him down in the wheelchair with
a soft push. John growled at the orderly. "You be careful
with Stan. We want him back alive." Then his natural
suspicion came out. "Hey sonny, what floor's this therapy
room on?"

The wizard started to pull the chair. "It's on the roof. By
the solarium."

Stanley was giggling before they arrived at the door. "Rupert, where'd you get the outfit, man?"

"Quiet," Rupert said, wheeling him into the corridor. "I
stole it from a laundry closet."

"What about the chair?" Stanley said, shaking the arm-
rests.

"That I got from the nurses' station."

"Out of sight . . . Rupe, the detectives in there, they
would've shot your face off if they figured you was Rupert

the lollipop. They got no brains. But they were nice to me."

They found a ramp that took them to the main floor. Rupert ordered nurses and hospital men about. His official gruffness seemed to cut through the illogic of a boy leaving St. Bartholomew's in a wheelchair, with plaster on his fingers and toes, and pajamas. Rupert spilt him into a taxi cab by angling the wheelchair against the door. The cabby wanted to fold the wheelchair for the boys. "Leave it," Rupert muttered. They bumped across the flatlands of Corona. The exhilaration was gone. Thinking of Esther, the boys grew morose.

The cab was alive with static that rubbed off Stanley's knees; he couldn't snuggle into the upholstery without suffering little electrical shocks. Rupert seemed strange to him with sunken jaws. Up to a month ago he'd been Stanley's pudgy messiah. It was torture for Stanley to read a book (the English alphabet made him gag), but Rupert could pull meanings out of any text. He chased off instructors at Seward Park with his deliberations on Coleridge, Karl Marx, and Shakespeare's corpse. The world was suicidal for Rupert. He got Stanley to sense the polarities between Manhattan and Hong Kong. The rich climb higher, Rupert said, and the poor shake like roaches at the bottom of the can. They squeeze one another and die. Stanley tried to resist Rupert's attitude. "How you know Hong Kong?" he said. "You been there, Rupe?" The messiah sucked on his cheeks, which were fatter at the time.

"Schmuck, I want Hong Kong I look at you."

Stanley could have broken Rupert's ear. He could have taken off a nose with one hooked finger. He could have severed Rupert from his scalp, Indian-style, by pushing at the temples until this messiah felt the burn in his skull. He respected bookishness too much. He kept his fingers out of Rupert's face.

The messiah didn't fail. He discovered a locus for his cause: Isaac Sidel. The Chief had come back to Seward Park on Career Day to give the key address. Rupert pointed to the stitching on the great man's sleeve (Isaac wore his Riverdale coat). "There's the cunt who rules us all." Isaac sang about opportunity, about the openness of his Headquarters to fresh ideas, about the job of a detective in New York; he brought the pretty boy with him. He paraded Coen. The girls ogled in their seats. Blue Eyes was asked to show his gun. Rupert and Stanley shrank down inside their row. The venom passed from boy to boy; their tongues were raw.

The cab couldn't make it to Chinatown. Mott Street was clogged with celebrants. So they had to disembark on Canal. Rupert lent his body as a crutch. Stanley could only take short hops on his mittened toes. They approached Mott from Bayard Street. Firecrackers roared around their ears, puffing their faces with smoke and impossible noise. Rupert shivered with the deafness that invaded his head. Street dancers, wearing dragon masks with molded eyes and horns that reached the fire escapes, slithered behind the boys, forcing them into johnny pumps and the windows of fruit and vegetable shops. They laughed at the banners of the Pell Street Republican Club, honoring the New Year with slogans that had been shot through with cherry bombs.

With Rupert crouching low, they picked their way across the gutter and landed at the New Territories tea parlor, a hangout for gentlemen from Hong Kong. Rupert had to shove a bit. He seated Stanley at a counter decked with oranges and tangerines. No one smiled at the boys. Rupert began taking dollar bills out of his pocket. "Here," he said, crushing the singles into Stanley's pajamas. "I got to split. We can't be ten blocks from Isaac's office. I don't need detectives sitting on my tail."

Stanley scowled at the mittens on his fingers. "I wish I could help you, Rupe . . . give Isaac an earache that wouldn't go 'way."

"Ah, forget about it. Isaac's my baby."

Stanley felt a touch on his shoulder, and Rupert was gone. He shook off images of Esther by ordering shrimp balls and bean curd soup in strict Cantonese. Watching the Hong Kong bachelors with their rice bowls next to their chins, he realized the futility of his situation. He couldn't hold a fork (chopsticks would have crashed into his lap). The shrimp balls arrived. Stanley wouldn't grovel with his face on the counter, licking under the dough for pieces of mashed shrimp. He couldn't even drop the shrimp balls into his soup. Gesturing ferociously with his mouth, he was able to steal a cigarette. He smoked, leaning into the counter, trapped on his stool. He couldn't have gotten to the door by himself.

A line of faces peered at him from the window. One by one the faces registered a grin. Stanley thought of whiskered cats. These boys had short hairs stuck on their chins. They were the Snapping Dragons. Joey, Sam, Sol, and Marv could have been the names of Yeshiva boys. That's how Stanley figured. With a stiff-legged walk, their bodies knifed into the New

Territories café. The air turned thick with the fragrance of oranges and Hong Kong soap. The bachelors drew their knees together to accommodate the Snapping Dragons of Pell Street, who overturned napkin holders and mustard pots with a swish of their winter jerseys. The Dragons surrounded Stanley Chin.

"Aint this a trip. The man himself."

"How's it going, Big Stan? Do you still love all the 'round eyes'?"

"He looks sad without his lollipop."

Marv was the quiet one. He took a fork from the counter and scraped it against Stanley's thigh. The other three Dragons scrambled for silverware. Sam tried to force a shrimp ball down Stanley's throat. Joey fed soup inside the neck of Stanley's pajamas. They grabbed the dollar bills. Stanley had his weapons. He could whip at them with an elbow. He could rupture a Dragon with his teeth. But he couldn't maintain his balance. He fell off the stool going for Marvin's nose. The boys began to trample him. He had a heel in his kidneys. He was swallowing blood. Four Dragons stood on top of him. Then they got off. He heard them say "Mother." The winter jerseys floated out of his reach. Somebody had frightened them away.

Stanley couldn't find who his savior was. He saw strings of oranges. He peeked right and left. The café floor nudged the bones in his skull. The bachelors were sloppy with their rice. His mittens were dirty. His mouth hurt. Soon he was muddled in overcoats. Three men had picked him up. They could only be cops. Even with blood in his nose he recognized Isaac's blue-eyed detective, Manfred Coen. This cop had a way of creeping into Stanley's life. Blue Eyes, Stanley wanted to say. Bubbles came out. Rupert hates you, Mr. Coen. Manfred wiped the blood with an embroidered handkerchief. Stanley bit down on the handkerchief to release the pressure in his nose. He didn't want to sneeze blood on a camel's hair coat. Blue Eyes had tender pinkies. He could massage a boy's skin under a bloody handkerchief.

13.

Brodsky had been glowering at transvestites for the better part of an hour. He couldn't direct his rage at the Chief. Isaac scrounged on Times Square when he was due at Headquarters for a press conference to celebrate the recapture of Stanley Chin. Talk about sleuths. Isaac was the only cop at Headquarters who had the brains to guess where Stanley would run. A Chinese boy goes to Chinatown, Isaac announced, while Cowboy Rosenblatt had his tongue in his ass, shoving detectives through Brooklyn and Queens. Ten minutes after the dispatcher gave Isaac the news of Stanley's flight from St. Bartholomew's, a squad of "angels" led by Manfred Coen walked from Centre Street to Mott, scooped the lollipop out of a Chinese cafeteria, and delivered him to the prisoners' ward at Bellevue. And now Isaac the Just was sleepwalking on Eighth Avenue.

"Downtown, Isaac, that's where we belong. Why are you pussying up here?"

The Chief ignored him. He was looking for a girl. Honey Schapiro had fled the coop again, disappeared from Essex Street to rejoin her pimp. Isaac wasn't on an errand for her father now. Mordecai could play his own shepherd. Isaac wanted information from the girl. The Chief couldn't squeeze Esther out of his mind. Living with Ida and Marilyn in two congested rooms, he imagined Esther Rose sitting naked on a floor with her finger in a mayonnaise jar.

"Isaac, there she goes."

They trapped Honey Schapiro between two Cadillacs. She had eyelashes on with thick corrugations that couldn't have been contained in a fist. You could see the imprint of her crotch through the flimsy material of her skirt. "Screw," Honey said, seething at Isaac. "My father's man."

Five pimps, "players" in floppy hats and suede coats that brushed against their ankles, came down the block to rescue Honey. Ralph, her old protector, was one of them.

"Brother," he said, "why you annoying an innocent girl?" With four other "players" backing him up, Ralph could afford a touch of arrogance.

Brodsky interposed himself between Isaac and the "players." "This isn't a pinch. It's a friendly conversation between my Chief and Honey Schapiro. So walk away, or you'll lose your pimping hats."

Isaac snatched Honey up from the bumpers of the Cadillacs and deposited her on the sidewalk. "Tell me about Esther and Rupert Weil."

"Fuck you."

The "players" chortled under the protection of their hats. "Honey, have you ever been to the Bronx juvenile house? The lady wardens have ticklish thumbs. They turn girls into zombies. You'll wake up with a baldie head. The wardens like to explore with pliers. Do you know what it means to have a bleeding nipple?"

Honey was petrified. Her shoulders wagged.

"Give me Esther's pedigree . . . You must have grown up with Rupert. What's he like?"

Honey scratched around her eye. "What do you want from me? I never saw them get it down together. Rupe, he came out of the crib pretty weird. With a chessboard tattooed on his belly. Call that normal? It takes Rupert to pick a mama who's a bigger fruit than him."

"Did Esther say anything to you?"

"Yeah, she said I should save my cunt for the proletariat. Shit like that. Who asked her advice?"

The five pimps figured Isaac was a crazy man; why else would he interrogate a bimbo in the street? Brodsky had his own suspicions. Isaac was stuck on a dead girl, a lollipop who would have been happy to kill him. "Chief, it's getting late. Those crime reporters have no loyalty. They'll interview Cowboy if you aint there to satisfy them."

The First Dep's sedan remained on Times Square. Brodsky had to go inside the Tivoli Theatre to scratch around for Wadsworth, Isaac's milky nigger. The chauffeur came out alone. He popped his head through Isaac's window. "Wadsworth says he don't sit in police cars. He'll meet you in the lobby. That's as far as he goes."

Isaac sent the chauffeur into the Tivoli again. "Brodsky,

tell him I'm hurting today. I'm too nervous to breathe the air in a movie house."

Wadsworth sneaked into the sedan; he sat up front with Isaac, while Brodsky dawdled under the marquee, staring at the bosoms on a signboard near the ticket booth. Wadsworth kept hunching into his seat. He had the pink eyes of a captured flounder. He wouldn't greet Isaac in Yiddish, or English. Isaac had to speak.

"Wads, I wouldn't pull on your shirt without a reason. You know that. I need. The Guzmanns stole a corpse away from me. They're meddling in my affairs. I don't want their dice cribs, Wads. Let them gamble in peace. Just tell me where the local whore market is, the place where the Guzmanns can trade in all the little girls they snatch from the bus terminal."

Wadsworth wouldn't shift from his corner. He showed Isaac a crumpled palm. "Put a razor in my hand, why don't you, Commissioner? So I can slit my throat before the Guzmanns get the chance."

"Don't be foolish, Wads. I'm not looking for a bust. I'll lean on the whore merchants, that's all. The Guzmanns will never know who my source is. How could they? And why curse me with the title of 'Commissioner'? I'm just a lousy chief."

"Isaac, Zorro doesn't sleep with his ears in the ground. You tap his marketplace, and he'll know."

"Wads, the Guzmanns are creepy pimps. If they touch you, I'll stick their balls in a medical jar." Wadsworth didn't smile. "You have a big family, Wads. A boy with uncles and cousins living in city dormitories shouldn't be so particular.

Get what I mean? You can float out of my house, Wads, that's your privilege. But if Cowboy finds out you're no longer registered to me, he'll take away your seat at the movies."

"Isaac, the Guzmanns are angels next to you."

"I agree. The Guzmanns wrap their money in prayer shawls, but can they keep you out of the Tombs? I'm your friend, not Zorro. Remember that. Now give. What's the name of that whore market?"

"Zuckerdorff. It's an outlet for diseased merchandise. Seconds and thirds. Zorro rents the showroom every week."

"A dummy corporation, is that it?"

"No. You can get a blouse for one of your girlfriends from Zuckerdorff. Isaac, be careful with the old man. He's Zorro's great-uncle."

Brodsky drove the Chief to "Zuckerdorff's of Sixth Avenue," which was in the basement of a pajama factory on Fortieth Street, between Tenth and Eleventh. Zuckerdorff had no secretaries or shipping clerks. He was a man with handsome eyebrows and prominent bones in his skull. He must have been eighty years old. Isaac had to extricate him from a wall of haberdashery boxes. Zuckerdorff didn't take kindly to this intrusion. "Gentlemen, do you have a piece of paper from a judge? Otherwise leave me alone."

The Chief wouldn't go for his inspector's badge, so Brodsky had to pull out his own gold shield. Zuckerdorff laughed in the chauffeur's face. "Mister, I seen plenty of those. They're good for scaring the cucarachas."

"Isaac, should I bend his mouth?"

The Chief stepped around Brodsky to catch Zorro's great-uncle at a sharper angle. Plaguing an old man with bluish skin on his temples made Isaac bitter with himself. But he couldn't allow a tribe of Bronx pimps to laugh him out of his borough. "Zuckerdorff, if you're counting on Zorro, forget it. I eat Guzmanns in the morning. They're tastier than frogs' legs. So consider what I have to say. Either you shut Zorro out of your company, and forbid him to walk his whores through these premises, or you'll have to stack your boxes in the street. I can turn you into a sidewalk corporation faster than Zorro can pedicure his father's toenails."

Zuckerdorff hopped to the telephone. He dialed without looking back at Isaac. His conversation was quite brief. "Zelmo, this is Tomás . . . I have two faigels in my office . . . funny boys . . . cops with bright ideas . . . they like to threaten people."

Zuckerdorff tittered with a finger on his lip. The bones shook in his skull. "My friends, you'd better vacate the building. Because your badges are going to be in my toilet bowl in another minute. If you decide to wait, I can fix you some beautiful red tea."

Isaac wondered if the Marranos poured jam or blood in their teacups. He was more curious about this than the identity of Zuckerdorff's benefactor.

A man clumped into the basement. He must have thick soles, Isaac assumed. "What precinct are you from?" the man growled, without seeing Isaac. "Are you grabbing for the nearest pocket? I'll break your knuckles off."

Isaac recognized Zelmo Beard, a disheveled detective from the safe and loft squad. Zelmo stared into Isaac's eyes. His chin collapsed. His ears seemed to crawl into his neck. He waltzed in his baggy overcoat, toppling the wall of haberdashery boxes. Zuckerdorff had all the omens a seller of damaged blouses could need. He blinked at Isaac. This cop had a capacity for pure evil. How else could Zuckerdorff explain the explosion of blush marks on Zelmo Beard?

Zelmo began to genuflect near Isaac's thighs. "Chief, I didn't know the First Dep was interested in Zuckerdorff . . . he takes in pennies, I swear. Garbage deals. He's a glorified junkman."

"Zelmo, I thought you had more sense. Why are you out muscling for a family that's been a nuisance to my life?"

"Isaac, I couldn't give a shit about Zorro."

"Prove it. I don't want him finding any more outlets for his little girls. Wherever Zorro turns, you chase him, Zelmo, understand? You can start with Zuckerdorff. Hit him with summonses, sprinkler violations, the works. That way Zorro will know I'm sending him my regards. Brodsky, come on."

The chauffeur basked on Tenth Avenue. His boss had to be the greatest detective in the world; better than Maigret, better than the Thin Man, better than Cowboy Rosenblatt. Isaac the Just could destroy the Guzmanns and all their Manhattan links without raising his thumb. He carried honey and acid inside his mouth. He could bite your face, or purr you to sleep. "Isaac, the reporters, Isaac. You'll snow them out of their pants. Should I signal Headquarters?"

"Brodsky, we're going to Bellevue."

The sedan pushed east, Brodsky sulking behind the wheel. He hated hospitals with fat chimneys and raw brick. Isaac went up to his mother's room. He found his nephews in the hall, Davey and Michael. The boys wore their hunting clothes: Edwardian suits cut to the measurements of a child, stiff collars, and identical flame red ties. "Uncle Isaac, uncle

Isaac," they screamed, lunging at him. Isaac had to bribe his nephews with fifty-cent pieces before they would give up their hold on his knees. The hallway would soon be a battlefield. The boys were waiting to pounce on their father. Where was Leo's ex-wife? Davey and Michael couldn't have plunked themselves outside their grandmother's door.

"My father's a killer man," Michael said.

"Who's he been killing?"

"My mother and me."

Isaac couldn't argue with a seven-year-old. He abandoned his nephews for a peek at his mother. Sophie had her vigilers: Marilyn, Leo, and Alfred Abdullah, her suitor from Pacific Street. Abdullah greeted Isaac with a sorrowful smile. An American Arab out of Lebanon, he could grieve over Sophie's wounds as hard as any son. Isaac nodded to the chairs around the bed. His mother lay in her pillows with blue salt on her lips, fluids leaking in and out of a nest of pipes. Marilyn barked a husky hello. Isaac felt uncomfortable with his daughter in the room. He saw the strain, the nervous flutter of her eyelids. She was miserable without Coen. And Isaac had contributed to this. Blue Eyes was only two flights away, in the prisoners' ward, minding Stanley Chin. Marilyn couldn't get through; the prisoners' ward didn't entertain the guests of jailors, nurses, or cops.

Leo could feel the chill between father and daughter. He edged closer to Marilyn's chair. Marilyn was his buffer zone. He remembered Isaac's promise to tear off a lung if he refused to give up his hiding place in civil jail. Leo hadn't made preparations to leave Crosby Street. The climate suited him. He could smoke, play cards, sneak out to visit his mother.

Sitting next to Marilyn, he waited for Isaac's wrath to fall. He'd misinterpreted the Chief. Isaac was too occupied with Rupert, Esther, and the Guzmanns to worry about one of his own simple threats. Leo's tenure at Crosby Street didn't concern him now. Abstracted, with leaking pipes in his eye, he spoke to Alfred Abdullah. "How's Pacific Street?"

Abdullah stared past Isaac in alarm: Sophie's head came off the pillows. "The baby," she said. "Bring me the baby." Sleeping, she had the look of a woman whose skin was on fire, her face deepening with blue salt and the passage of blood. Coming out of a coma, her complexion changed. She was pale, with a mouse's color, during her periods of lucidity. The glass pipes swayed over her arm, impeding the flow from gooseneck to gooseneck. "Bring me the baby," she said.

Isaac stood with both fists in his chest. Abdullah made little grabs at his throat. Leo covered his eyes. Only Marilyn had the sense to clutch the pipes and narrow their sway. "Jesus Christ," she said. "Can't you see? Mama's calling for Leo."

Leo sprang out of his chair. His shoulder landed in the bed. Sophie began to caress his bald spot. Leo was crying with his mother's fingers in his scalp. "Shhh," she said. "Where's the philistine?"

Abdullah crouched behind Leo. Sophie rejected him. "Not you," she said. "Where's the philistine? . . ."

"Mama," Isaac said, his ankles sinking under him. "I'm right here."

"Did you meet the cock-a-doodle?"

Isaac shrugged, rendered incomplete by his mother.

"The cock-a-doodle," Sophie insisted. "In Paris, France."

Isaac was caught with pimples on his tongue. Leo must have snitched; mama couldn't have known about his rendezvous with Joel in the Jewish slums of Paris, unless the fluids dripping into her also fed her intuition.

Sophie was through with bald spots. She reached for Abdullah's hand. Leo wouldn't move; he kept his ear against Sophie's hospital shirt. Sophie smiled.

"Alfred, are you making a living?"

Abdullah answered yes.

"Good. Because I aint putting out for paupers."

Devoted to her, Abdullah didn't reveal his embarrassment. Leo drew his ear away from the bed. "Mama's getting delirious," he whispered into Marilyn's shoulder.

"Isaac, are you fucking lately?"

"Mama, who has the time."

Leo twisted Isaac's sleeve. "Don't answer her . . . Isaac, her brain is swelling up. Do you know what it means to be without a husband thirty years?"

Sophie dropped into the pillows. Her mouth twitched once. Her eyes registered a certain confusion. She tasted the salt on her lip. She belched. She tumbled into a profound sleep, holding Abdullah's hand. Leo crept out of the room.

Trapped between Abdullah and Marilyn, Isaac grew shy. He couldn't belittle Sophie's quest for boyfriends, in and out of her comas. No sugar leak could kill his mother's sexuality. Her skin was turning deep again. Isaac was left with his daughter. He heard bitter screams from the hall.

Leo was wrestling with his ex-wife. The elusive Selma lay under his knees, breathing sporadically, with Davey and Michael climbing up their father's back. "Let me finish her once

172

and for all," Leo choked out, his voice edged with a violence Isaac had never encountered in his brother. Leo wouldn't acknowledge Michael's clawing fingernails. Davey was sitting on his neck. Leo had his knuckles in Selma's windpipe. "Do I have to suffer on account of you?" Isaac had to pluck Davey and Michael by the seat of their Edwardian pants before he could get to Leo.

"Go back to your jail. Leo, the guards will miss their pinochle without you."

Leo stumbled towards the exit, nurses, patients, and visitors popping out of doors to stare at him with loathing in their eyes. Davey and Michael blinked scowls at their father. Selma began to writhe on the floor. Spit collected under her nose. "He ruined my insides . . . oh, my God . . . oh, oh." Selma grimaced and squeezed her ribs. "Help me, nurse, nurse." The boys leaned over their mother, battle-weary, but terrified of the snaking motions of her body. Isaac understood Selma's scam. Her sputum was clear; he couldn't find a fleck of blood. Her cries had too much rhythm. He bent down, curling over Selma, so the boys couldn't hear him. "On your feet, sister-in-law. This place doesn't carry collision insurance. If you're thinking of hospitalizing yourself, here's my opinion. Some of the wards have handcuffs hanging from the beds. Sister, I'll lock you in. This is Bellevue, remember? People have been known to wander for years in the crazy ward."

"Fuckface," Selma mouthed into Isaac's chest as she fixed her stockings. The boys witnessed Selma's miraculous rise. They hugged her, pushing Isaac off with mean little blows.

Marilyn smiled from her grandmother's doorway. Isaac was plagued by a swarm of relatives, like any Jewish patriarch. He

173

supplied the family glue. The Sidels would have crumbled long ago without the ministrations of Isaac. He soothed, he slapped, he mended broken wires, Marilyn's incredible daddy.

❖

The crime reporters wanted their conference in the Police Commissioner's rooms, where they could peek at the furnishings of an old commissioner, Teddy Roosevelt; draperies, a gigantic desk, portraits of Teddy on the wall. Isaac wouldn't allow it. He herded the reporters into his own office, which had no marble fireplace, no chandeliers, no maroon on the windows, no desk with historic chinks and scars and a spacious hole carpentered for the knees of a future president of the United States, and could only remind such men and women of their ancient, cluttered "news shack" on Baxter Street. Isaac wouldn't provide sandwiches, or a police captain in a handsome tunic to coddle the reporters; Brodsky became his press secretary. The chauffeur clucked behind Isaac with envelopes belonging to the lollipop case.

The Chief talked of Rupert and Stanley's Chinatown escapade in primitive style, without embellishments, winks, and anecdotes, or the mannerisms of Barney Rosenblatt (Cowboy loved to rattle his cufflinks at reporters). Brodsky didn't hear the scratch of a single fountain pen. Cradling their notebooks, the reporters stood with slanted heads. The *Times* man was the first to jump on Isaac. Could the Chief enlighten him? What did the First Deputy's office make of isolated rat packs such as the lollipops preying on old men

and women without real cause, devoting themselves to sense-
less destruction?

"It's a worldwide phenomenon," Isaac said, cuddling his
chin. "The same thing is true in Paris. The French police
can pull any master criminal out of a chart, but it's teenage
bandits—lollipops—who are taking over the Champs-
Elysées. Babies robbing banks. Without a name or a face.
Some Billy the Kid with a cheap kerchief on his nose."

"Or Robin Hood," said Tony Brill, the fat man with
credentials from *The Toad*; neither Brodsky nor Isaac had
ever noticed him at Headquarters.

Isaac frowned at this *Toad* man, ignoring Robin Hood.
"Eight-year-old muggers and rapists in New York," he said.
"Killers at nine and ten. Are we supposed to keep infants in
our confidential files?"

The stringer from *Newsweek* had a passion for intelligence
tests. He led Isaac away from abstract causes, and asked him
to fish through the envelopes in Brodsky's hand. "Chief, you
must have a sorry bunch of detectives doing research for
you. Where's your fact sheet on Rupert Weil?"

Brodsky grew miserable fumbling inside the sleeves of
different envelopes. The stringer was already smug. "What's
the kid's I.Q.?"

"Two hundred and seven," Isaac said, making Brodsky
close all the sleeves.

The *Daily News* man began to titter. "The kid must be a
genius. I hear Mozart only came in at a hundred and ninety-
nine."

"Two hundred and seven," Isaac said.

The stringer was obstinate. "What about Esther?"

"She went to parochial school," Isaac said. "Her teachers are

Spagnuolos, suspicious people. They refused to supply us
with any records. But I don't have much faith in intelligence
quotients. They tell you very little. Rupert was a chess player
once. He could have been a grandmaster, who knows? He
gave it up at twelve. Was it 'intelligence' that told him
where to place a knight? Look at Bobby Fischer. He has an
I.Q. of a hundred and eight or nine. So give me a theory about
geniuses? I'm not begrudging Rupert's terrific score. But *his*
genius comes from willfulness, from a maddening obsti-
nancy, not a talent for checking the right box. Take my word.
Your geniuses come narrow these days. They have the power
to stare at an object, a piece of fruit, a man's heart, and block
out everything else in this stinking world."

The reporters hadn't anticipated philosophical notions
from a police inspector. The two nice ladies from the Brooklyn *Squire*, who were partial to Cowboy Rosenblatt, considered it an odd turn of events that Stanley Chin and Sophie
Sidel should land in the same hospital. Was Isaac slinging
mud in Cowboy's eye? Had the caper at St. Bartholomew's
been staged for the benefit of newspapers and magazines?
Was Rupert Weil working for the First Deputy's office?
Did he steal the Chin boy at Isaac's request?

"Pure coincidence," Isaac muttered. "Stanley has nothing
to do with my mother now. And it's a crazy idea to think that
Rupert works for me."

"Not so crazy," said Tony Brill.

"What do you mean?"

"Nothing. . . ." Tony Brill had to retreat from Isaac's
terrible glare. *The Toad* couldn't insure him against potholes
and loose bannisters at Police Headquarters. "Chief Sidel,

weren't you friends with Rupert's dad? Maybe the kid was trying to find a subtle way to cooperate with you."

"Bullshit," Brodsky said. The members of Isaac's rubber-gun squad peeked into the room. Because they didn't have pistols at their hips, the reporters mistook them for civilians, and figured they could be rude to ordinary clerks. The rubber-gun boys were waving frantically at Isaac, without a bit of color in their cheeks. Brodsky mingled with them. His pants began to slide under his belly. He had to grab his pockets to save himself. "Conference dismissed," he croaked with a tight mouth.

The reporters piled out of Isaac's office, dissatisfied with the surreptitious moves of First Deputy men. Isaac remained with Brodsky and the rubber-gun boys. "What's wrong?"

"Isaac, a package came to you . . . from Rupert Weil. We called the bomb squad. They're bringing over a special dog to sniff it out. It could be a booby trap."

"Dummies," Isaac said. "I don't need a lousy dog."

It was wrapped in butcher paper, with heavy string on the outside, the kind of string a bialy maker might use to secure a bag of rolls. It was a tremendous package, over two feet high. Isaac couldn't bite through the string; the fibers were too coarse. Brodsky ran for a pair of scissors. Isaac snapped at the knots. He tore under the butcher paper. The rubber-gun boys could see the rounded edges of a hatbox, a hatbox with a name on it: Philip Weil. Isaac opened the box. Brodsky put his hands over his ears. Isaac's other men slinked to one side. They saw a hand rustling in crumpled newspaper.

"Isaac, what the fuck is it?"

He held a chesspiece, a black bishop made of wood, with

the points of a miter sitting on top, an inexpensive piece out of Rupert's own collection. The rubber-gun boys were bewildered. The package confirmed Rupert's craziness for them. Isaac wouldn't offer his opinion. He chased out all his men. "Brodsky, close the door."

Isaac fingered the chesspiece, all the undulations in the wood (Rupert's bishop had a swollen belly), the weak black paint that was beginning to bald, the strip of velvet at the bottom, the rough spots along the miter. Rupert's telling me something, Isaac muttered in his head. The present of a bishop couldn't have been a caprice. Was the boy challenging Isaac to a game of postal chess? Should Isaac counter with a bishop of the opposite color? No. Rupert wasn't into that. This chess piece had to go back to his father's game. Philip was a master with a pair of cooperating bishops. He always drew black against Isaac, giving him a clean advantage. Isaac had the opening move. Philip wouldn't sit on his pieces. He eschewed the normal lines of defense. Philip had to slap at you. He didn't gobble up your pawns, or badger your king into slow strangulation. While you attacked with an armada of knights and rooks, your pieces sailing on some grandiose mission, Philip crept around them and used his bishops to tear out the throat of your queen.

"He's after one of my ladies," Isaac spit into the hatbox. How many queens could a cop possess? Three or four? Rupert's going to slap me like his father did. Isaac couldn't believe the boy would touch Sophie again. But the Chief had a cautious heart. He'd put another "angel" outside Sophie's door in case he slipped over Rupert's logic. Was it Isaac's wife, the baroness Kathleen? Rupert would have to dig her out of the Florida swamps, Kathleen's new dominion. Ida

Stutz? What could Rupert want with Isaac's fiancée? "Marilyn," Isaac said with a definitive nasalness. It had to be.

The dog arrived from Twentieth Street, where the bomb squad had its own kennels on the roof of the Police Academy. Isaac was expecting a German shepherd with brilliant ears and a very long nose. This one was a mouse, a snip of a dog, a cocker spaniel with stunted legs and a body that hugged the ground. Isaac could pity such a creature. He wouldn't send it home to Twentieth Street without a sniff inside the hatbox.

The prisoners' ward at Bellevue had a ping-pong table, old-fashioned sandpaper rackets, and a bag of dusty balls, perfect for Manfred Coen. He could pass the time slapping balls into the table. There were only three patients in the ward today: a black Muslim with a wound in his thigh, a deranged Puerto Rican car thief who tried to hang himself in a police station, and Stanley Chin. None of them was in proper condition to play Coen. But the little pecking noises coming off the sandpaper were beginning to make them twitch. Stanley had to shout from his bed to halt Coen's slaps. "Blue Eyes, you wanna play?"

Coen laughed. "You'll hurt your fingers, Stanley. You can't grip a bat."

"I don't need no bat." He waved a mitten in the air. "I play with this."

"With your cast?" Coen said. "The doctors would skin me alive."

"How they gonna know? Blue Eyes, don't be afraid."

Coen found a wheelchair. He pushed Stanley from the bed to the ping-pong table, setting him up so his chin would be near the table's center mark. Coen picked up the racket. He wouldn't angle it. He didn't want to confuse the boy with side spin off the sandpaper. He stroked the ball over the net. Stanley punched it back with his left mitten. Coen lunged with his knees wide apart. He missed the ball. He frowned at the sandpaper and took another ball out of the bag. He blew on it, testing the seams by mashing it into the table with his palm. He listened for the dull pock that would have told him there was a crack in the ball. The pock didn't come. He served again. Stanley punched the ball with his other mitten. Coen knocked his knees together. The cop was astonished. His racket kissed nothing but air. Stanley had developed top spin with the plaster on his knuckles.

"That's kung-fu, man."

Stanley put a mitten in his mouth. He couldn't stop giggling. He hadn't meant to tease Coen, but the cop's disgust with the racket in his hand could make a boy piss with his eyes. "It's called the iron fist. It takes concentration, man. You aim for one spot. Sometimes it screws up, Mr. Coen. But when you hit the ball, it stays hit."

An orderly motioned Blue Eyes over to the telephone. Manfred was still confused. How could a boy in a wheelchair with mittens on destroy his game? Coen wished he'd brought his sponge bat, his Mark V, to the prisoners' ward. Then he'd discover what an iron fist could do against a few millimeters of sponge. Brodsky was screaming at him.

"Coen, you deaf, or what?"

Manfred wiggled the receiver. "Brodsky, I can understand every word."

"Then move your ass over to Headquarters."

"What about Stanley Chin?"

"Forget the little Chinaman. Coen, bring your piece. If you drop a bullet on the floor the First Dep will murder you. It's Rupert Weil. I think Isaac wants you to blow him away."

Part Four

14.

———————

Marilyn could hear the wind in the struts of her daddy's fire escape. The radio promised a blizzard. She shuddered at the prospect of blinding snow. Marilyn was a Riverdale girl. Snowstorms could make her crazy. She remembered the blizzards out of her childhood, when Riverdale was blocked off from the rest of the world, and she couldn't go to school. She had to live on peas and sesame sticks in her mother's cupboard. She would see puff balls on the Hudson, the wind rolling loose masses of snow. Her mother was in Baltimore, or Miami, and her father was caught downtown. Isaac couldn't telephone. The snow had strangled the wires. Crackles came out of the telephone box, a disgusting electric snore. And Marilyn would suck on her braids, exhausted, the peas growling in her belly, too frightened to cry.

She couldn't even laugh at her ancient hysteria, anxieties that were fifteen years old. She was in her daddy's house.

After three husbands, she hadn't outgrown her fear of rotten weather. She could call her mother in Florida, beg Kathleen to soothe her with tales of soft Miami, winters without a peep of snow. Marilyn was ashamed to dial for Florida. Kathleen would pull her outside weather reports, and Marilyn would have to pick through all her marriages, provide Kathleen with details of husbands two and three. Somebody was knocking on her father's door. Marilyn opened up.

A snowman had come for her, Manfred Coen with white eyebrows and blood-red ears. Marilyn could adapt to such a snowman. She didn't ask him impertinent questions. She shook the icicles off his camel's hair coat. She set his trousers on the radiator cover. She gathered up the ends of her skirt so she could rub his eyebrows with warm material. She put a turban made of washcloths over his ears. The snowman didn't have the sense to wear galoshes. She got him out of his shoes. She wrapped his feet in Isaac's towels. The snowman gave a sneeze.

"It's a witch's tit outside, a whore of a day."

"Chauvinist," Marilyn laughed. "Can't you think up a few male items? . . . like scummy snow, or a witch's balls. How did you get past Isaac?"

"I didn't have to." The snowman blinked. "Isaac sent me over."

Marilyn's chin rose off the snowman's knees. "Then this wasn't your idea? You arrived because of Isaac?"

"Marilyn, that Rupert kid's been reaching out. Isaac says he's after your throat. You need a bodyguard, and Isaac figured . . ."

"Get out of here."

Marilyn threw her hairbrush at the snowman. She ripped the turban off his ears. Coen hopped on Isaac's linoleum.

"Fucking Blue Eyes, don't tell me what Isaac figured. Isaac figures shit. Don't you ever do your own bidding? Errand boy. Damn him, first he keeps us apart, and now he pimps you over to me. What's he going to come up with next? Does he want me to put out for the whole Police Department? Tell him a girl can get awful choosy about her dates. I'll try a new pimp if he doesn't watch out."

"Marilyn, maybe it wasn't so evil. Isaac knows how much you'd hate having a cop around . . . he thought he could make it more bearable if the cop was me."

"Coen, take your pants off the radiator and put them on. I don't fraternize with bodyguards."

Coen went for his trousers. He got one leg in before Marilyn wrestled him down onto Isaac's daybed. He could feel the tremors in her fist, the squash of her thigh, the frenzied weight of her attacking body. She was all over him, elbows, breasts, and knees. Coen wouldn't defend himself. Marilyn spent her energy beating up a snowman. Her old hysteria had come back. She was stuck in Riverdale again, with blizzards in her head, implacable snow walls between Manfred and her. She didn't recognize the cop; pure blue eyes couldn't bring her out. Marilyn was immune to hypnotic specks of color. She felt a hollow in the snowman's chest; she crawled inside.

Marilyn awoke with a blink that worked itself into the roots of her nose. She could smell a man's flesh. She wasn't naked, no, but she was out of her skirt. Blue Eyes had turned her into a papoose. She was tucked to the bed in a woolly blanket. She could barely move her arms. "How long did I nod off?" she said.

"Maybe an hour," Coen answered from the radiator. He had a fat lip, scratches on both sides of his face.

"Was I awful to you?"

"Not so bad." The scratches wiggled out when Coen smiled. "But I had to tie you down. You were thrashing pretty hard."

He loosened the blanket for her. "I'm sorry," she said, fighting back the urge to touch Coen's lip. "I always freak out before a big snow. . . . Manfred, sit with me."

Coen sat across from her, mindful of the storms she could conceive with her elbows and a swiping finger. "Marilyn, I would have come without a push from Isaac. I was trying to sneak away. He had me running into corners. He bounced me to the end of the borough. I couldn't eat a meal sitting down. I followed the moon skipping for Isaac. Then he locks me inside with Stanley Chin. I was sleeping with ping-pong balls."

"Shh," she said. "You don't have to explain." She crawled up to Coen's knees. She must have become a witch in her father's bed. The scratches on Coen's face were arousing her. She wanted to lick the wounds she'd made. It wasn't out of gruesomeness. Marilyn didn't have the instincts of a torturer. She was raw to Coen. She'd murder her father if it would save Blue Eyes. Crazy thing, she couldn't have exposed her feelings for him without marking up his cheeks. Coen was still babbling.

"Marilyn, I should have stalked Rivington Street, snatched you coming off the stairs, pulled you uptown. Kidnaping is my specialty . . . only it had to be outside. He's my boss. I couldn't invade Isaac's premises."

She would have pounced on him with the affection of a woman who'd outgrown three husbands, but she knew this would scare him off. Coen was suspicious of her. She had to move slow. She reached around him with her neck and kissed the swelling on his lip. It wouldn't have been a proper strategy to take off his clothes. Marilyn pecked outside his undershirt. She sucked on an ear. How do you wake a snowman?

Coen was coming alive. He blew spit into the spaces under her cheekbones. He nibbled the shells of her eyes. He wouldn't grind at her with his trousers on. The cop had gentle ways. But she could feel his prick through the gabardine. His tongue began to snake into the corner of her mouth. The wetness chilled her teeth. Her armpits bled a powerful water that was like no ordinary perspiration. Coen had sweetened her with his tongue in her face. Marilyn wasn't used to such slow kissing. "I could love you, Manfred." She had nothing more to say.

Headquarters was besieged with copies of *The Toad*. Someone, presumably Tony Brill, had piled them on the front steps, indifferent to snowballs and the mud on a cop's shoe. Cowboy's men must have been the first to gather up these wet copies. Twitching with thoughts of revenge, they distributed bunches of *The Toad* to every floor. Brodsky sat outside Isaac's office with a muddy newspaper on his hips. The chauffeur was incensed. That fat worm Tony Brill cluttered the second page with photographs of Rupert Weil, and an exclusive report on the three lollipops. Rupert was snarling at the camera, in the overstuffed uniform of a housing cop.

Brodsky couldn't read without moving his lips. *The Toad* offended him. A rag, Brodsky concluded, a goddamn hippie rag for pinkos and society whores. He had never seen such a mishmash of swearwords and bleeding type. Tony Brill talked of children's crusades, lollipop wars, and the martyrdom of Esther Rose. He accused Isaac of "fucking the brains of all New York." To amuse his readership he'd scratched a primitive cartoon of Isaac pissing on Delancey Street. Pictures that mocked his Chief (Isaac had flabby testicles in the cartoon) couldn't make Brodsky laugh. Brill was a maniac. He swore Isaac had ruined, or was about to ruin, Philip Weil, Mordecai Schapiro, Seward Park High School, Honey Schapiro, Cowboy Rosenblatt, Stanley Chin, Esther Rose, the Puerto Rican people, the Spagnuolos of Brooklyn, the citizens of Chinatown, and Manfred Coen (Brodsky chortled at the mention of Coen). Only Rupert had escaped him, and Rupert was making war. Who else but a lollipop, said Tony Brill, would have dared represent the grievances of his borough?

Brodsky knocked on Isaac's door. The Chief summoned him inside with a dreamy hullo. Isaac had to be hatching a plot, or gruff noises would have come down on Brodsky's shoulders. The Chief was sitting with *The Toad.* Brodsky seemed reluctant to interfere with the traffic in Isaac's head.

"Isaac, should I attend to Tony Brill? It's a ripe time. People can drown in snow."

"Leave him alone," Isaac muttered. "He can't hurt us."

Then Isaac came out of his gloom. "The kid'll make me notorious. They'll tremble when I across the street. Didn't you know? Crime disappears wherever I walk."

The chauffeur had trouble with Isaac's twisting speech. He felt obliged to titter. "At least let me do something. Isn't *The Toad* on La Guardia Place? Isaac, I could sabotage their press. It's easy. They'll have to print with crayons and rubber bands."

The Chief was putting on his slipover. He didn't liven to Brodsky's plan for wasting *The Toad*. Isaac was superstitious about journalists. You couldn't kill their stories. If you took their print from them, they'd write on the bark of a tree. Cut off their fingers, and they'll spell with a nose.

"Isaac, don't you want your limousine?"

"Never mind. I'll walk."

"Eighteen inches, Isaac, that's what they predict. The car has snowshoes. Why should you wet your feet?"

Isaac met a few "crows" on the stairs. They leaned into the bannisters to give the Chief some clearance. None of them would whisper "Tony Brill" in his face. Even a "crow" might not survive one of Isaac's bearhugs. They needn't have worried. The Chief was into his own head. He stepped on a "crow's" foot without excusing himself. The problem was Marilyn. With Rupert sending bishops through the mail, Isaac had no cheap solution. Should he strap her to his shoulder, take her everywhere with him? Or find a cubicle for her in the women's house of detention? He had to rely on Coen. Marilyn would have bitten off the tongue of any cop or matron Isaac could provide. Now he'd have to move into Ida's place. His own detectives would laugh at him; they'd say Coen had dispossessed him, bumped him out into the street.

Brodsky was wrong about the snow. Eighteen inches? Isaac felt a thin powder under his shoes. He noticed a man on the sidewalk through the haze of falling snow. Isaac thought he could recognize the grim shoulders of Jorge Guzmann. He wasn't in the mood for a heavy embrace. Isaac looked again. It was Gula One Eye, his old nemesis.

"Gula, you'll catch cold. They're predicting a hurricane."

Gulavitch couldn't talk without eating some snow. "Isaac, you should have blinded me twice. It wasn't smart. I'm your enemy. Why did you leave me with a good eye in my head?"

Isaac didn't have to slap Gulavitch's pockets: the old man wouldn't carry a weapon other than his extraordinary thumbs. Still, Isaac had to get him out of here. If the "crows" spotted him, they'd squeal to Cowboy Rosenblatt, and Cowboy would arrest Gulavitch for blocking the sidewalk. They'd take him down to the cellar, make him pose without his eye patch, call him Isaac's idiot.

"Gula, don't you have to peel potatoes for Bummy? Go to East Broadway. Bummy needs you."

The old man licked snow off the top of his lip. "Isaac, I got plenty to peel. Your nose, your eyes, your mouth."

Isaac hailed a patrol car coming from the garage on Mulberry Street. The driver squinted through his window. He couldn't understand why a big Jewish Chief would be hanging around a retard with snow on his face. But he didn't question Isaac.

"This is Milton Gulavitch. He's a friend of mine. Take him to Bummy Gilman's on East Broadway. It better go smooth. Milton doesn't like bumpy rides."

Isaac walked to the Garibaldi social club. He didn't bother peeking over the green stripe in the window. He went inside.

This was a poor hour to annoy Amerigo Genussa. The landlord was making pasta for the Garibaldis. He had his own witchery. Amerigo could transform the club into a trattoria with a few mixing bowls, crumbled sausage, anchovies, green and white spaghetti, walnuts, Parmesan cheese, and a pepper mill, bunched around the club's espresso machine. The landlord had niggardly counter space. He was obliged to hop from bowl to bowl, with a wire beater in his chest.

Isaac didn't wait for overtures from Genussa. "Landlord, I told you once. I don't want your stinking goons near Essex Street."

Amerigo continued to hop. The beater would fly into a bowl with little turns of the landlord's wrist. He dealt with Isaac only after the froth began to rise. "Did I invite you to dinner? You've been copping too long. I mean it. Your manners are in your ass. I don't hire degenerates. All my men have families. It looks funny to me, Isaac. You have the best detectives in the world, and you can't catch a Jew baby. So it's up to us."

"He's my property, Amerigo. You won't enjoy your spinach noodles if your friends cross the Bowery one more time."

Isaac heard the wicked suck of the espresso machine. Cappuccinos couldn't tempt him now. The landlord sprinkled walnuts into a bowl.

"Go scratch yourself," he said, walnuts dropping out of his fist. "Isaac, don't tell me how you're going to torture us with the FBI's. Newgate's a prick, just like you."

Isaac shoved a helping of walnuts and anchovies into the nearest bowl. His hand came out stiffened with egg white. The Garibaldis glowered from their tables. The landlord smiled.

"Play, Isaac. You can be the new macaroni man. No cock-sucker's going to provoke me into a fight. The City pays you to kill. Wait . . . be careful at the corners, Inspector. You could get run over by a bicycle thief."

Isaac couldn't blame Amerigo too much. The landlord had to avenge the old people of Little Italy for the trespasses of Rupert Weil. But Isaac wouldn't tolerate baboons peering into the windows of Puerto Rican and Jewish grocers. The snow was thickening on Mulberry Street. An enormous Chrysler cruised behind Isaac. The Chief scowled at the car.

"Brodsky, who told you to hang a tail on me?"

The chauffeur stuck his head outside the Chrysler to gape at Isaac and spit a few words into the snow. "Chief, the dis-patcher's been paging you for fifteen minutes. Wadsworth bought it in the neck."

"With a slug?" Isaac said, getting into the limousine.

"Isaac, there aint a hole in the nigger's body. It must have been a crowbar."

The Chrysler hugged the ground with the help of Brodsky's miracle "snowshoes," tires that could climb walls and stick to any ceiling. They weaved around ordinary sluggish auto-mobiles and arrived at the Tivoli Theatre in under ten min-utes. The theatre had already been roped off. Patrolmen in high galoshes and yellow raincoats kept civilians outside the rope and planted "crime scene" placards behind the ticket booth. Brodsky had to hold his belly while he ducked under the rope. The lobby was swollen with homicide boys and "crows" from the Chief of Detectives' office. Isaac paddled between them. He didn't have to fish for the corpse. Isaac's milky nigger was huddled over a chair in the middle of the orchestra, surrounded by a small band of detectives. He had a blue hump where his neck was broken. His eyes stared out of his skull. His tongue was in his shoulder. "Jesus," Brodsky said, with the taste of puke in his nose. He put his hand over his mouth and ran for a drink of water, his trousers falling to his knees. The chauffeur had flowered underpants. The skin on his thighs was pale white. One of the detectives turned to Isaac.

"Any ideas, Chief?"

"No," Isaac said.

"I thought the little nigger belonged to you."

"So what," Isaac growled. "Get him into a goddamn body bag. I don't want him lying around like that."

"Isaac, have a heart. We can't interrupt the investigation. We'll bag him soon as we can."

The police photographer was on his knees snapping pictures of Wadsworth from different angles. Two "latent" experts dusted the chairs in Wadsworth's row. The man from "forensic" was busy chalking the outline of Wadsworth's body, the exact fall of his arms and legs. Isaac had scant respect for these laboratory freaks. Chalk marks made pretty clues, but they couldn't sniff out a murderer for you. Brodsky came back from the water fountain. He whispered in Isaac's ear. "It was a crowbar. I'm telling you. You can't twist a human being like that without a piece of iron. Look, they gave him a hunchback."

Isaac couldn't see the bite of any metal; Wadsworth had no scrapes on his neck. The "crowbar" was Jorge Guzmann's elbow. He walked out of the Tivoli, Brodsky chasing after him. "Isaac, don't leave me behind."

"Why not? I don't need you until tomorrow."

The chauffeur shuffled on the sidewalk. "Isaac, what should I do?"

"Talk to yourself. Sit in the car. Read a porno book."

Isaac trudged to Tenth Avenue in search of Zorro's great-uncle Tomás, the haberdasher who dealt in seconds and thirds. The snow had begun to penetrate Isaac's shoes; their tongues were growing wet. The haberdasher had a tight cellar door. Isaac wouldn't fiddle with locks today. He toppled the door with a heave of his shoulder. Zuckerdorff wasn't alone. A Puerto Rican gunsel sat with him, a killer from Boston Road. Isaac raised the gunsel by the tufts of his sideburns, carried him around the cellar until a rusty pistol and a roll of quarters in a handkerchief spilled out of the gunsel's shirt. Then he placed him gingerly at Zuckerdorff's feet. The gunsel was in agony. He had a torn scalp from this loco policía. "You pull on my brain, man? You crazy motherfucker." Isaac booted him behind Zuckerdorff's chair.

The haberdasher put his head in his lap, leaving Isaac to stare at blue veins on a chiseled skull. He's older than my father, Isaac realized. The Chief hid his compassion from Zuckerdorff. "Uncle Tomás, your grandnephews have committed atrocities in my borough. They murder innocent men. If Zorro wanted a neck to crack, he should have come to me."

Isaac couldn't vent his fury on blue veins. He attacked Zuckerdorff's haberdashery boxes, kicking them with his snowy shoes. The boxes crumpled around Isaac; he buried the gunsel under a pile of smashed lids. Zuckerdorff didn't move. Isaac stubbed his toes. He found no murderers inside a box. Isaac was the guilty one. He fed Wadsworth to the Guzmanns. He allowed his own feud with Zorro to compromise his stoolie. He'd forced Wadsworth to reveal a piece of information that could only point back to him. Like a schmuck, a police animal, he'd turned Wadsworth into expendable merchandise. The Chief was through with boxes. He kicked his way out of Zuckerdorff's cellar showroom.

❖

Ida wasn't fickle with her best customers. She put paprika in their cottage cheese. But her mind wasn't on blintzes and petty cash. She forgot to shave the celery stalks. The spinach bled into the egg salad tray. The dollar bills sitting in the register turned orange from paprika thumbs. The dairy restaurant wasn't used to such shabby tricks. What could Ida's bosses do? They were helpless without this horsey girl.

Ida Stutz was seeing snow, not pishy water, a mean Manhattan trickle, but dark Russian snow, the kind that could swallow lampposts and suffocate a pack of wild dogs. The Ludlow Street professors had to blow into their split-pea soup. None of them could get Ida out of the window. The girl had her nose in the glass. Let her dream, the professors advised. She'll get pains in her calves. And then we'll have our Ida. They smiled when Ida shook, tearing at the flesh on her hips. They figured she was coming back to them. It wasn't so. Ida saw a face on the other side of the glass, the face of an uptown savage, with harsh lips and rubber cheeks, a chin that dandled in and out of a bullish neck, piggling eyes, and a pumpkin's ingrown ears. Ida ran out of the restaurant.

"Isaac, did you lose something uptown? Maybe your life?"

She didn't think a man could sweat with snow in the air.

The Chief was burning up. Ida scrutinized him. Poor inspector, he has engines that work overtime. "Where are you going, Isaac? That isn't the way to Rivington Street."

Do powerful engines make you dumb? The Chief kept marching towards Broome Street. "Your place," he mumbled with his big teeth.

"Isaac, how come?"

"Marilyn has a guest."

Ida fell in behind him. She wasn't frail. She had her own combustion machine. "God bless that Marilyn of yours, is she keeping company again? A fourth husband?"

"No. I put him there. One of my detectives. Coen."

Ida didn't enjoy his abbreviated talk. Does a simple "Coen" solve everything? She knew about this handsome cop. Why was he throwing Blue Eyes at his daughter? She couldn't pluck more words out of him. The Chief had sinking shoulders. She tried to take him by the hand. He slapped at her fingers, Isaac the snarling bear. "I can walk," he said. She'd have to feed him honey at home.

Ida lived on the sixth floor. The Chief was hugging bannisters. He could be exhausted by a flight of stairs. Ida pushed. The Chief arrived on her doorstep. She poked her key in the lock. Ida didn't bother with herself. She fixed a tub for Isaac, with perfumed bubble water from a town in Roumania. It said so on the box. She undressed him, got him out of his slipover, sharkskin trousers, and holster straps. She tested the bath with a whirling finger under the bubbles. She sat him down in the tub. She combed his sideburns. She brushed his teeth with the clear toothpaste that came as a sample in yesterday's mail. She couldn't find Isaac's scrotum.

The Chief was shriveled up. He blinked at her with a hooded eye.

"Take off your sweater, Ida. It's warm in here."

She brought him brown honey in a tablespoon. Isaac took the honey in one lick. He rose out of the tub, refreshed. Was the bear ready to dance? Sweet Isaac, he had foam on his pectorals. Ida blotted him with the inside of her sweater. The Chief was playing with her clothes. Buttons snapped under the pressure of a thick hand. Isaac was into her cups; he could nurse a nipple as well as any other man. The brassiere dangled at her side. Isaac was on his knees. He had her navel in his mouth. The suction on her belly produced an incredible shiver. Ida couldn't hold on to her legs. She crashed into him. He fell back with Ida, but he wouldn't come out from her belly. Ida thought she would have to pee. Her thighs contracted with the force of a mule. She couldn't throw the Chief.

"Don't stop, Isaac. Please don't stop." But she could feel his mouth begin to drift. Her belly was no longer occupied. He wouldn't graze her with his tongue, nuzzle the walls of her chest. It was Isaac's turn to shiver. The bear had blood between his toes. Uptown bruises? She should have explored him better in the tub. Ida wasn't alarmed. She would rub off the anxious spots. She stroked the bumps of skin behind his ears.

15.

THE prisoners' ward at Bellevue suffered a whiteout. Its windows were going blind. Snow packed into the spaces between the grilles, and froze to wood and glass. Stanley Chin was tripping out on the hard blinks of snow in the windows. Rupert Weil was full of shit. Only a tilted brain would compare Hong Kong with New York. There were no white storms in Kowloon. None of the orderlies would lend him a cigarette. They were asking fifty cents a smoke. Stanley wouldn't trade with robber barons. He had a quarter in his pajama pocket. He wished Blue Eyes would come back.

The ping-pong table was growing bald without Detective Coen. The net had droops in its bottom line. The balls were getting yellow. A shrill song from the edge of the ward drove Stanley into the slats of his hospital crib. The noise was spooking him. He hadn't heard a telephone ring since yesterday night. Bellevue was supposed to be snowbound. "Hey Chico," he said to the orderly on call inside the prisoners' room. "You told me nobody could get through. What's happening?"

"I dunno," the orderly snapped. His eyes were red from staring into blind windows too long. "Maybe it's the Holy Spirit."

The orderly picked up the phone. "Yeah, yeah . . . speak louder, huh?" He plucked a portable wheelchair from the wall, opened it, climbed in, and wheeled himself to Stanley's crib. "The ding-a-ling, it's for you."

"Who is it?"

The orderly laughed. "Your favorite boy. Blue Eyes. You got luck with that cop. You must be a special customer."

The orderly lowered the slats, but he wouldn't give the wheelchair over to Stanley. "Let him wait. You don't want him to think you're an easy lay."

"Chico, I got a quarter in my pocket. Take it, and push me to the telephone."

The orderly reached into Stanley's pajamas, stroked the quarter, flushed it out, and made Stanley climb into his lap. He paddled them both around the ward at a reckless clip, bumping off bedposts, shaving walls, heckling the other prisoners, who were groggy with snow, then slid out of the wheelchair, and left Stanley with the phone in his elbow. Stanley had to dig with the side of his face to clutch the earpiece. "Mr. Coen?"

He heard a horrible buzz, scratching that had a murderous resonance against his jaw. Then a giggle came through the wire. "It's me."

"Rupe?" Stanley was befuddled, but he turned away from

the orderly to shield the voice of this crazy giggler. "Chico said it was Blue Eyes."

"Schmuck, how could I give my real name? Would they let Rupert Weil call Bellevue? Blue Eyes gets you anywhere."

The static began to suck at Stanley's cheek. "Rupe, the hospital's closed to the world. They can't find milk for the babies. The nurses go 'round asking prisoners for blood. How'd you make the call?"

"With my middle finger. You know another way to dial?"

"Don't sound on me, Rupe. I got warts in my ear from the telephone."

"Ah, I'll pull you out of that dump. Not today. I'm running errands for my father."

"Who does errands in a storm?"

"I'm going to fuck Lady Marilyn."

Stanley burrowed his head into the earpiece. "Rupe, what'd you say?"

"I'm going to fuck Isaac's daughter . . . in the face."

The phone spilled out of Stanley's elbow and knocked into the wall. "Chico, could you bend down for a guy?"

The orderly scooped up the phone. "Hey man, send Blue Eyes a kiss and say goodbye."

Stanley grabbed with his cheek; the static could burn holes in a boy's mouth. He dropped the telephone. Rupert wasn't there. The orderly dumped him into the crib. "Chico, write a message for me . . . please. It's important."

"Write it yourself. We got a union, man. I aint your slave."

Stanley wagged his plaster mittens. "Would I bother you if I could write? . . . I'll give you a dollar."

"I touched your pocket, man. You aint got no green."

"I'll owe it to you. Don't be scared. Blue Eyes will pay."

The orderly leered at him. "Is Coen into sponsoring rats?" He unclipped his ballpoint pen, twirled it in his mouth for a second, and started doodling on the back of a hospital menu. "What's the message?"

Stanley was reluctant to recite his dread to the orderly, but he had no choice; he couldn't buy wheels to Manfred Coen. He hadn't been asleep at St. Bartholomew's. The detectives who guarded him reviled Coen. They also hated Isaac and his daughter, whom they called a skinny cunt. Stanley learned from them that Blue Eyes was in love with Marilyn. He wouldn't snitch on Rupert, but he didn't want Coen's girlfriend to die. So he dictated to the orderly: "Dear Detective Coen, please watch out for Marilyn the Wild. She'll be in big trouble if she opens her door tonight. Sincerely, Stanley Chin."

The orderly scratched out an I.O.U. Clamping the pen to Stanley's mitten, he forced him to sign his name. The signature was a series of bumps. "It goes to Police Headquarters," Stanley said. "Blue Eyes will pay you more than a dollar."

The orderly smiled. Leaving Stanley, he shoved the message through a slot in the prisoners' iron door, placed his tongue in the peephole, and whispered to the guard on the other side of the door. "Freddy, you see that paper. Stuff it in the toilet, fast. It's a poison-pen note from the lollipop gang."

The orderly had a horselaugh behind his fist. He wasn't worried about the I.O.U. Stanley would have to pay up with a little skin, blood, or Bellevue chocolate pudding.

❖

Rupert was stuck inside a telephone booth at the corner of Essex and Grand. A quartet of goons from Little Italy, fellows in long coats who had been stalking Rupert for a good two weeks, drifting in and out of grocery stores, restaurants, and horseradish stalls, eating bialys and kosher pickles, were standing on a snowbank in front of the booth. They rubbed shoulders to stay warm. All four of them carried odd bits of Amerigo Genussa's plumbing tools: lead pipes to pin back Rupert's ears, a metal snake to twist out his eyes, wrenches and screwdrivers to play with nostrils and lips. Rupert cursed his rotten luck. He'd have to huddle in the booth until the goons picked another snowbank. Rupert had no shirt on under the coat he had stolen from the housing police; his nipples were about to freeze to the lining.

He dialed Headquarters to badger Isaac before the goons disappeared; he got a recorded voice that whispered husky things to him. Rupert couldn't understand a word. He had weapons in his pocket: a fork, a spoon, a blunted can opener. They were sharp enough to go under the skin of a woman's neck. He would undaughter Isaac with the push of a spoon.

"Mister, once in your life you'll know what it means to lose."

Rupert held no grudge against Lady Marilyn. Being Isaac's daughter was a question of circumstance; her one misfortune was Isaac himself. And Marilyn would have to pay for that. Rupert was no ordinary butcher; Philip's boy wouldn't have been able to bleed a duck, or a cow. But he had to take something from Isaac that was more valuable to him than his own police inspector's skin. Rupert wasn't unmerciful. He would bleed Marilyn faster than Isaac had bled Philip and Mordecai, and the whole East Side.

Rupert had all the cunning of an Essex Street coyote. From the stairwells and soft walls of abandoned buildings he learned how to live on the fly. He always kept a source of nourishment somewhere on his body. Ruffling his coat, he pulled a yellow lollipop out of the sleeve. Esther had been addicted to lollipops, and he caught his sweet tooth from her. He watched the gorillas on the snowbank and manufactured some yellow spit. The lollipop disabled him; yellow spit could only suck up images of Esther. Enclosed in a booth, with a candy brick in his cheek, he flashed on Esther's bosoms. He was smelling Esther Rose, feeling the stripes of fuzz on her back. He had to crumble the lollipop, or go silly in the head.

He jumped out of the booth. The shivering of the door must have reached the snowbank. The gorillas turned their heads. They were much too cold to make a significant leap. Girding themselves, they began to plod after a hopping overcoat.

Mordecai Schapiro faced snowstorms with cucumber slices, schnapps, and a lick of salt. These were the limits of his appetite. He was grieving over his daughter Honey, who couldn't stop running away from him. Would she catch pneumonia in such a thick porridge of snow, with her short skirts and flimsy stockings? Why should he kid himself? His daughter was a whore. She walked the streets in all kinds of weather. A strict professional, she even had a manager, a pimp with a silk handkerchief, Mordecai supposed, and a card saying she was free of the crabs. The schnapps mingled with the salt on his tongue, and the cucumber eased his bitterness, the pain of a father who felt mislaid.

Mordecai had a guest. Only a moron would visit you in the middle of a squall. He opened his door to a phantom in Cordovan shoes. A Manhattan snowdrift couldn't influence Philip Weil's queer sense of fashion. Philip came in his church clothes, Scotch plaids and tight gloves. Always the dapper hermit, in Mordecai's estimation. Their friendship had soured over the last twenty years. Without Isaac to cement them with his bearish charm, they slipped apart.

"I didn't expect you, Philip. I would have prepared. But it's hard to shop in a storm. I hear the A & P is out of goods. People hoard, you know. They want to safeguard their deliverance. You can't blame them. If you're old, you remember the hard times. And if you're young, you have a brutal imagination."

"Don't be alarmed, Mordecai. I didn't come to steal your salt herring. Tell me about Honey. Has Isaac found her yet?"

"Isaac's a big man. Why should he help me twice in the same month? He drinks tea with commissioners. He rides in limousines. He knows the best opera stars."

"So he isn't perfect," Philip said. "He can still find Honey for you."

"Sure, stick up for him. He could have saved Rupert, but he didn't. I begged him. 'Isaac, go to Philip. Philip needs you.' Does a Chief listen? He has special wax in his ears to make him deaf to old friends."

"That's how a policeman survives. He shuts out certain noises. Do you expect him to redeem every wandering boy in New York?"

Mordecai glowered at the fineries of Scottish wool. "And how do you survive? Philip, it interests me. You sit home morning and afternoon. You can get pimples on your ass from so many daydreams. It's no picnic sorting mail in a post office, but it keeps me occupied."

"I don't daydream, Mordecai. I watch soap operas, I browse in Rupert's library, I play handicap chess against myself, I polish my shoes. My mornings aren't dull to me."

Mordecai despised talk of handicap chess. He couldn't tolerate Philip's eccentricities today. But he smiled at the joke in his head. "We're dunces," he tittered out. "We could have put together a small family of Schapiros and Weils. What's wrong with arranged marriages? Rupert and Honey. They wouldn't have crept so far."

"Why curse fifteen-year-olds with marriage?"

"Hypocrite, your boy wasn't sleeping with that Yeshiva girl? Everybody knows the Sephardim are a little crazy. They're more Arab than Jew. Did you want *that* in your family?"

Mordecai was ranting to an empty room. Philip had gone back into the storm. "Fuck him," Mordecai said. "He's too much of an aristocrat to fight with me." But Mordecai couldn't find much solace in his schnapps. The cucumber was pulpy in his mouth. He wouldn't get through the winter without his girl. Let her be a whore, he reasoned flatly, staring at the buttons missing from his robe. Whores can manage a needle and thread, whores can sew. Mordecai was exuberant. If enough pimps died in the storm, Honey would have to come home.

❖

Cowboy Rosenblatt couldn't withdraw to the Rockaways, where he was keeping house with a Polish widow who owned a chain of hardware stores. There were no exits out of Manhattan that Cowboy could use. Rows of abandoned cars blocked every bridge, and the subway lines into Brooklyn couldn't unsnarl themselves; no train got beyond Flatbush Avenue.

The Chief of Detectives had made provisions for the storm: he wore his thermal underwear. But it couldn't exempt him from the wind that howled through his suite of offices, rattled his many drawers and his great supply of lamps, hurled pencils off his cabinets, toppled wastepaper baskets, and bit into his secret files. The lamps began to twinkle around 8 P.M., and Cowboy's office went dark. He groaned his way to the outermost room, calling for some lieutenant with a flashlight, or a match. "Where is everybody?" he shouted. "Son-of-a-bitch."

He strolled out on the landing, clutching the bannister rail. Dark stairs couldn't intimidate him, a man with two guns, a superchief, three thousand detectives under him. He was dreaming of his Polish lady, and the empire of bolts and nuts he would soon share with her, Rosenblatt the hardware king. He felt a shiver in the rail. Cowboy was no mystic; wood didn't shiver on its own. Another policeman had to be moving up or down the stairs. A match sputtered near Cowboy's thighs. He saw a pair of cheeks in the shadows, a burrowing forehead, the broad nose of Isaac the Just. Cowboy fondled the pearl on his Colt. He could have shot out Isaac's eyes.

"Isaac, you shouldn't walk these steps without an escort. God forbid, you could fall on your face. Where's Coen?"

Isaac let the match go out. Cowboy leaned into the bannisters.

"Push me, Barney. I'd love the ride. But remember I have a gun next to your ribs. It sits at a funny angle. If you shake me hard enough, it could explode in your groin."

"You're an animal, Isaac, that's what you are. My family comes from a line of cantors, all holy men. The Rosenblatts raised three synagogues in Brooklyn alone. You, Isaac, you suck garbage in the street."

Isaac brushed past him without uttering another word. Cowboy kept to the rail. Where could he go? Should he run to the cellar and kibbitz with the fingerprint boys, or throw himself into the storm and tunnel a path to the property clerk on Broome Street? He decided to stand still. Tinkering with Isaac brought him to the subject of daughters, Isaac's and his own. The Chief of Detectives was crawling with lecherous ideas. He had an insane urge to make Marilyn the Wild, get inside her clothes, chew her nipples, scratch her armpits, drop sperm between her eyes. He'd avenge his daughter's ugliness on Marilyn's body. Cowboy had to grub through Brooklyn locating a husband for his Anita, nab a struggling bachelor older than himself, wed his last daughter to a man with rotten teeth and a swollen prostate, while cunty Marilyn flew from her husbands and had an affair with Manfred Coen. The world wasn't right. Cowboy had been passed over by whichever angel distributed charity to fathers in the boroughs of New York.

A hand swished against his jacket. Cowboy jumped. A flashlight snapped on. It was one of his "crows."

"Boss, what are you doing here?"

"Idiot," Cowboy said, "I'm airing my pockets," and he took the flashlight away.

❖

Rupert plunged from snowbank to snowbank. His progress was minimal. It took him half an hour to go from Essex to Orchard Street, two skinny blocks. He couldn't see the end of his thigh. He would sink down to his hip pockets with every forward push. He had to wiggle with all his might to rise out of the snow. Rupert was disappointed in the Mulberry Street gorillas. They couldn't keep up with a growing boy. He shook them without having to disguise the stab of his sneakers. He left tracks in the snow that an elephant could follow.

Not all of Rupert's plunges were successful. He landed in a snowslide that carried him off his feet. He couldn't get out of the drift. At ten miles an hour he could carve a path with his ears. Coming into a patch of firmer snow, Rupert held on, and found himself overlooking the signboard of Melamed's Grand Street department store. Rupert was amazed at the fury of moving snow; he must have flown twelve feet off the ground. The signboard couldn't be any lower than that.

The wonders of a snowslide began to wear off. Rupert became depressed. Melamed's reminded him of his former struggles, when he and Esther had been put at the mercy of a store detective, maybe a month ago. They were shopping for clothes in Melamed's underwear department. Rupert made a little belly for himself, stuffing boxer shorts under his shirt. Esther was the brazen one. She squeezed an entire load of lollipop pants through the neck of her blouse, and toured Melamed's with a hump on her back. A short rabbi with curling sideburns and a black religious coat, who had been sifting through the barrels of underwear together with Rupert, came behind Esther Rose, mumbling "Pardon me," and clapped a handcuff on her wrist. Rupert gawked at him. The rabbi tugged, his politeness gone. "Girlie, shake a leg, before I tear your arm off."

The rabbi dragged her up three flights to Melamed's detention cell, a cage about four feet high, designed to humiliate shoplifters, forcing them to live with their shoulders bent, while the assistant manager called the police. Rupert stalked the cage, testing the thickness of its wire mesh. The rabbi plucked off his sideburns and shed his religious coat, coming into the natural grubbiness of a store detective with tobacco between his knuckles and spit on his tie. Rupert couldn't pierce the mesh. Esther screamed, with her forehead under the detective's ribs. "Daddy, I have to pee."

"Pee as much as you like," he said, muggering at her. "You aint coming out."

Shoppers began to collect around the cage. Esther dipped her thighs and peed. The shoppers backed off, their mouths widening with disgust as Esther's urine streamed towards them. The detective couldn't be swayed. The urine traveled under his leg in two long fingers. "You'll wipe it up, sister. With your tongue."

Esther unbuttoned her blouse. The shoppers crept back to the cage, standing in pee to gape at a shoplifter's nipple. The detective skipped in front of Esther, screening her with his arms; even a touch of nudity in the cage might cost him his job. He unlocked the cage door and prepared to handcuff Esther again. He shouldn't have turned his back on Rupert. As Esther moved into the door, her blotchy, pissed-over skirt clinging to her thighs, and her neckline plunging below her bosoms, Rupert dug his teeth into that portion of the detective's heel resting outside the hump of his shoe. The detective howled, losing the handcuffs, grabbing at his wounded foot. He was still in Esther's way. She had to tweak his testicles before she could slip between him and the cage. The shoppers had never met such a vicious girl. They pinched their bodies in to avoid fouling themselves with Esther. She shoved Rupert towards Melamed's escalators, helping him bounce off the metal tips of the stairs. Esther wasn't finished with Melamed's. She had more lollipop pants and a huge, impractical girdle when they arrived at the main door. Esther hadn't gotten off totally free. It took a week for her shoulders to unbend.

Rupert crawled to a different snowbank. It was easier to launch himself with his fists. Having no gloves, he stretched the sleeves of his coat. Rupert enjoyed the heights; the snow was mushier near the ground. He could see into living rooms, touch the fire escapes, eat a crisp hunk of snow. Crossings didn't matter to him; traffic lights blinked their colors. Rupert snuffed at the warning signals. He was perfectly safe on Grand Street. Cars and buses couldn't ride over a mound.

Crawling with abandon, snow in his eyes, he bumped into the window of a live poultry market. Rupert was a vegetarian. He despised the smell of roasted flesh. The idea of meat darkening in a stove made his gums twitch. The only flesh Rupert would have nibbled on was Isaac's. No lie. He'd have gone cannibal for Isaac the Pure.

He saw young roosters, hens, and rabbits in the window. The roosters were the lords of the market. They lived two in a cage, while the hens were piled four and five deep, sitting on each other's back, some of them picking at their own necks until bald areas emerged above the wings. These chickens disgusted him. He watched the pink-eyed rabbits, white and gray, chewing lettuce, sniffing for their water trough near the edge of the cage. Their coats seemed incredibly soft. Rupert wanted to stick his thumbs in the fur, stroke their pink eyes to sleep. Who the hell would eat a rabbit? he argued to himself. The transom over the window wasn't snug. Rupert could squeeze a knuckle inside. He began clawing at the space between the transom and the window bar. His knuckles were growing raw. He rubbed them in freezing spit. The transom couldn't worry him. He was three fingers into the market.

Squirming, wedging with a shoulder, he raised the transom high enough to slip through the glass. The chickens squawked. The roosters wagged their fleshy combs with a sad pull of the head. Who had castrated these birds, fattened them, groomed their combs for marketing? The bunnies blinked their noses in terror of Rupert. It was dark in there, the snowbank ending just below the transom, allowing a meager peck of light. Rupert had to deal with so many eyes. He walked on his toes to calm the hens. He funneled bits of corn into the roosters' mouths, getting scratches on his hand. He felt the pulse in a white rabbit's pink wet nose. He wished for Esther. She would have loved a live rabbit under the blanket, nudging against her skin. What would the bunny do when Rupert and Esther went down together on the blanket? Rupert stopped. He could hurt himself with blanket dreams. Tasting Esther put smoke in his skull, made him recollect how much Isaac had stolen from him. Rupert preferred a bunny with a drier nose.

✢

Brian Connell shouldn't have budged from the station-house. No one would have blamed him for sleeping in the locker room during a hard snow. But he had to redeem himself. He undressed the big Jew's daughter, fed her whiskey in a bar, fucked her, and sent her home to Blue Eyes. The cunt had snitched on him. She cried rape, rape, and now the First Dep's killer squads were gunning for Brian Connell. How do you duck an "angel" with a sharpshooter's ribbon? Brian had one means of escape: catch little Rupert before Isaac takes his revenge.

He'd been stalking Rupert's grounds, from Clinton to West Broadway, in Bowery clothes that were beginning to rot. He had a few appendages today; a silk scarf that he wore on his face, and hunter's boots from Abercrombie's to protect his delicate ankles from snowbite. The wind imposed hallucinations on him. Rabbits were crossing Grand Street. It had to be devil's work, or a mirage caused by the particular slant of falling snow. He kept a medallion in his pocket from the Holy Name society. But rubbing a piece of cold metal couldn't scare the rabbits away. They would come and go between the nod of an eyelash. Brian was terrified. He'd have to surrender his body to a Catholic nursing home, or move out of the state. Run to Delaware and join his cousins on a skunk farm.

He couldn't ignore the squabbling in the snow. There was a rooster near his legs. This was no pale beast, fickled over by a storm. The rooster had wattles and a red hat. Brian chased after the stupid bird; it rushed between his Abercrombie boots. He flopped in the snow, unable to keep up with a chicken. He noticed a man skulking on the opposite side of Grand Street. Brian drew his gun. The man was trying to stuff the rabbits in a shopping bag. Brian called to him. "Sonny boy, stay where you are."

The man hurled the shopping bag; a rabbit flew out. Brian fired over the man's ears to prove that you couldn't throw shopping bags at a city cop. A hill collapsed behind the thief. "Come out with your hands in the sky."

He heard a loud slapping noise. His own hill of snow was disintegrating under his boots. The thief had a gun in his hand. Brian dove into the tires of an abandoned truck. He squinted around the tires to shoot at the rabbit thief. He could feel dull, trembling pocks in the snow. The guy had to be holding a cannon on him, or a Detective Special. Nothing else could make holes like that. The man was waving a yellowy object. Brian shuddered when he recognized the indentations of a gold shield. "Prick," the man said, coming out of the snow. "I'm from the Second Division. Who the hell are you?"

Brian was too weary to sniffle. The sergeant would slap his eyes with paper work. Brian would be typing forms in triplicate until his fingers dropped off, explaining why he had the urge to blow skin off a detective's ears. They'd flop him for sure. And Isaac had all the authority in the world to kidnap Brian, feed him to the rat squad, who would nibble on his ears, suck his lifeblood away, sneak him out of the borough, and deliver him to Ward's Island in a box, before the snow disappeared. The property clerk would claim his Smith & Wesson. Brian could look forward to a wet grave, and the anonymity of a policeman buried without his gun.

"Are you nuts?" the rabbit thief said, shaking Brian out of his gloomy visions. "You shoot at a man for finding pets in the street? Bunnies are dumb. They could die in Manhattan. I was bringing them out to Islip, for my kids."

Brian shrugged. "Dangerous," he said. "Lollipops . . . I'm looking for Rupert Weil."

❖

All things returned to Isaac. Isaac was the freezing river, the rock, the snow. Isaac was the sewer under Grand Street, the snot in Philip's handkerchief, the dust on the wings of Mordecai's nose. Isaac was the holy warrior who swept Philip and Mordecai under with his good deeds and gutted Esther Rose, who sleeps in the vulva of his daughter and gets his nourishment from the pubic hair of a fat blintze queen. . . .

Two men were following Rupert while he speculated in the snow. These weren't the Mulberry goons. They didn't have long overcoats. They were dressed like foreigners, it seemed to Rupert, in softer clothes: sweaters, earmuffs, and wool hats. It was hard to appraise their look in a storm, but Rupert could swear they were brothers. Their faces had a cunning that didn't respond to the snowbound shops of Grand Street. The brothers might be slow in commercial matters, in geography and arithmetic; they walked with a mental twitch, as if they were moving into strange territories. They couldn't be connected to Isaac; they were much too awkward for a team of cops.

Rupert didn't bother trying to shake them; he'd ride under their fists, if he had to. He'd wrap the earmuffs around their eyes. He'd bite the wool on their heads. They couldn't grab Rupert off the snow. He cut into Allen Street, but the wind drove him back. He had to burrow with his knees, dig his way

around the corner. The trip exhausted him. He winked at the
sweater boys, whose tits were covered with snow. Woolly
heads were no match for Rupert Weil. He had a spoon in his
pocket, a spoon that could gouge a path to Lady Marilyn, or
splinter the cheeks of an enemy. He revived, watching the
earmuffs labor. The brothers were stuck. They couldn't make
Allen Street. Rupert dismissed them as Brooklyn refugees.
He was clear to move at a pace that was convenient for him.
He had ice on his toes, and his nipples had turned blue. He
put a hundred yards of crawling between himself and the refugees. He fell over a hand. "What is this shit?" A foot wiggled
out of the snow. Rupert pulled. An old man emerged, hugging
bits of snow to his body. He'd been buried alive, without
galoshes or a scarf. Rupert rubbed the old man against his
coat. "Who are you? Where do you live?"

The old man pointed to a building. "I was going for a
knish," he said. "A kasha knish. It's foggy out. I can't see."

"Do you have a wife?" Rupert asked.

"I live with my daughter. The knish was for her."

"This aint knish weather, if you ask me. All the delicatessens
are closed. Come on."

The storm had tailored the old man's building, cutting it
off from its own ground floor with a snowbank that was
humped up like an elephant's back. Rupert charged into the
hump, searching for an entrance to the building. He slapped
out a crooked furrow with his hands and feet, and brought
the old man inside. The building was chillier than the snowbank. "That's a greedy girl," Rupert said, huffing for warm air.
"I'd kasha her nose for her, but I'm in a hurry."

Coming out of the furrow he'd made, he was snatched up
by four long overcoats. His enemies, the gorillas of Mulberry

Street, had been waiting for him. They spotted Rupert as he stalled to unbury the old man. They banged his arms with their lead pipes, menaced his eyes with their plumber's snake. "Go quiet, little pest, or we'll divide you into twenty packages. You have an appointment with Amerigo Genussa."

Rupert struggled in the snow, unable to reach his can opener, fork, or spoon. The plumber's snake ripped into his eyebrow. He was sneezing blood. He had pipes in his shoulder-blades. The refugees arrived, the sweater boys, the brothers wrapped in earmuffs and childish hats. Was it snow, or blood, that was beguiling Rupert? How could four gorillas be off their feet? Only one brother battled with them. Pipes bounced off the head of this refugee. He could tear a whirling metal snake with his fingers. Take two gorillas into his chest with a single arm. Hug the color out of a man's face. Rupert heard the crunch of bone under the long coats. The four gorillas had rubbery knees. They twitched and groaned near the second brother, who said, "Jorge, that's enough."

He attended to Rupert's eye with spit on a paper napkin. "I'm César Guzmann. Some people call me Zorro. That's my brother Jorge. Don't blink. You'll get snow in your eye."

"Why are you following me?" Rupert said, growing surly.

Zorro pecked at the blood. "Be polite. I don't care for myself. But you'll offend my brother. The good fairy sent us to watch out for you."

"I fight with my own elbows, Mr. Zorro, thank you. I'm Rupert Weil."

"We know that," Zorro said, finishing with the napkin. "We buried your lady, Esther Rose. My father hired two cantors to sing at her funeral. The best songs you can find in Latin and Portuguese."

Rupert peered out of his bloody eye. "What was Esther to you?"

"A Ladina without a decent grave. Nothing more. We had a friend in common. Big Isaac. He should be in the ground, not your lady."

The gorillas slithered away from Rupert and the Guzmann boys, with lumps in their overcoats.

"See," Zorro said. "It pays to keep you healthy. Could you torture Isaac if they took your elbows off?"

The Guzmanns were delicate people. Zorro wouldn't have introduced himself without bearing trinkets from his family; he stuck a hand through the neck of his bottommost sweater, his fingers moving like giant pimples under the wool, and dragged up an ice pick and a tiny handgun in a square of dirty cheesecloth. "My father wants you to have a choice. You can dig into Isaac, or blow his tongue away. Don't worry about the pistola. It can't be traced. It bites hard for a .22. Drop it near Isaac's feet and run."

Rupert shrugged at the offerings. "I have my tools, Mr. Zorro." Were the Guzmanns out of their minds? He couldn't keep from staring at the refugees, who walked into a storm bundled up like chubby snow gods to rescue him from a pack of goons. "Are you a Brooklyn boy, Mr. Zorro?"

"Never," Zorro said, making grim pulls with his chin. "We come from Peru. Remember, you have a place to hide. My father can get you into Mexico City, Bogota, Lima, or the ten Little Havanas in the East Bronx. Just ride the train to Boston Road and ask for me."

He signaled to Jorge. The brothers fixed their earmuffs and went into the snow with shuffling knees.

❖

Coen had feathers in his mouth from Isaac's mushy pillow. Marilyn wouldn't let him out of bed. He was unbridled now, minus his holster and his socks. The blizzard had simplified their lives; no interruptions from Isaac for thirty-six hours. Rattling fire escapes couldn't frighten her with Blue Eyes in the house. She licked him clean, until he lost the nervous shivers of a cop. She wasn't a dreamy girl. She understood Coen's obligations, his loyalty to her father, his somber ways. She hadn't slept with too many orphans before Coen. She wouldn't have believed a man could hold his dead father and mother in the furrows of his chin. He had a deathly feel. His lovemaking was profoundly beautiful and slow. He didn't spit. He didn't nibble on her ear with an obscene patter, like her second husband, and her early beaus. He moved in her with the rhythms of a somnambulist, a drugged devotion that pinned her to the walls of Isaac's flimsy mattress and made her squeal.

She felt like Isaac, who could taste paradise every night by putting his nose in a honey jar. That's how greedy she got with Coen. She wanted him to nuzzle her until her orgasms traveled to her fingers and her eyes. "Mother God," she said, thrown back to her church days when she had to confess the crime of liking to touch her own bosoms. "Make me come, Manfred, make me come."

At rare intervals she'd climb off the mattress to fix a meal for Blue Eyes and herself; she clawed into the heart of her father's lettuce, dropping chunks onto a plate, with cucumbers and a dip of garlic, onions, and cottage cheese. Marilyn was worried about the blandness of this feast. She couldn't vary the menu in a blizzard. It was cottage cheese, or starve, because the refrigerator had been stocked by Ida Stutz. But there was a little red wine in a goosenecked bottle, and they sipped at it judiciously, conserving the bottle, in case they had a visitor. Isaac might come through the window; he had a passion for fire escapes, and he hated climbing stairs. Let her father fly in! Marilyn wouldn't blush. She was old enough to be caught naked with a man. Isaac must have seen her tits once or twice during the short tenures she'd had with her three husbands. He didn't complain. Marilyn wasn't her father's deputy. She'd sit him on the window if he badgered husband Coen.

She decided not to skimp with the bottle. She poured wine over Blue Eyes, into the trenches of his body, collarbone, elbows, kneecaps, the line of blond hairs that split his chest, the grooves around his balls. She was planning to devour Coen, drink the wine off her new husband, catch him with her tongue. She fell into his shoulder, caressing him with her forehead and her jaw, while Coen shut his eyes, grunting like a dead man, wind coming from his lungs in low, even squalls, and Marilyn cursing all the wedding rings she had worn, the bridal veils, the embroidered sheets of honeymoon hotels.

Rupert's bad eye was beginning to close. He had to sight unnaturally, with his cheek jutting into the storm, or bang out a path with his knees. He bumped along, enduring the wind-burn on his lips, trying to figure Isaac's doom. He wasn't so resolute near Delancey. The traffic was dead. He had a whole boulevard to himself. He could have hopped across on the roofs of abandoned cars if that had been his wish. He wasn't in the mood to make a crooked metal bridge.

The window of a men's slack shop on the north side of Delancey had been smashed in the storm. He saw looters, men and boys in grubby coats, sacking the store; they carried great bundles of pants through the jagged teeth in the window. One of the looters, a *portorriqueño* with scars on his lip, swerved into Rupert, glaring at the uniform of a housing cop; he came up close to inspect the sneakers, the damaged eyebrow, Rupert's hairless face, and he smiled. "*Yo no sé*, man. There's plenty for everybody. Dig in."

Rupert wasn't interested in slacks, but the looters wouldn't let him go. His uniform was too valuable; he became their lookout. Rupert stood outside the window with a glum demeanor. He disapproved of anarchy done for profit. These slacks wouldn't cover the gang's own legs; they'd be sold at a thieves' market, or hawked uptown, with the looters turning their arms into clothes trees to display the wares. The leader of the gang was a gringo, like Rupert. He wore a stocking cap and an old Eisenhower. He noticed the condemnation in Rupert's narrow cheeks. "What's eating you, bro'?"

"Nothing," Rupert said.

"Then why you looking at me with unkindness?"

"Because I'd like it better if you stole what you need and went home."

Boys were coming out of the window who had to be runts, midgets, or creatures under ten. They bobbled under Rupert's neck, carrying their load of slacks in a line that ended with a blur of snow. This same line could have reached for blocks, Rupert understood. The runts might be marching straight to the Chrysler building. The leader took one of the loads off a runt and pitched it at Rupert. "You must be a rich man's kid," he said. "A mama's baby. You don't know shit about stealing."

Rupert ran for his life. He couldn't have fought an army of runts. The snow was pitted with obstacles and dangerous traps. He walked on crushed glass, smacked into the domes of submerged johnny pumps, skidded off the carcass of a frozen dog. He arrived on Rivington Street with a raw nose. Could he murder Isaac's daughter now? He was fortified by the lay of snow in the street. The storm had worked for him. There was a snowbank near the fire escape he had to reach. He could grip the bottom rung of the ladder without performing acrobatics under Isaac's window.

Rupert, Esther, and Stanley Chin had wasted whole afternoons spying on the window from a neighboring roof. They had seen Isaac slash like a bloated sea animal on top of Ida Stutz, his policeman's ass rolling in deep, tortuous waves. Such turbulence seemed comical to them. Rupert had to wonder how his own buttocks behaved while he was down with Esther. Did they slap in the air, waver high and low? Rupert wasn't a sea elephant. His thrusts had to be sweeter than those of Isaac the Pure. Before Esther died, he saw another woman in Isaac's window. It was Lady Marilyn. He'd come here alone to watch her shamble across the living room, or go into Little Italy with a shopping bag. She was a skinny girl. She didn't have her father's thick neck, or the complexion of a blintze queen.

Rupert walked up the hump of the snowbank. He was on the ladder, hands and feet. He climbed with his elbows in his chest. The going wasn't easy. He had to measure the distance between every rung, or slip down the ladder. The wind could be devilish at this altitude; it beat against Rupert's nose, lashed him into the rungs, the higher he got. He reached Isaac's fire escape with snow on his chin, his fingers swollen with ice. The fire escape shook as Rupert crouched onto the landing. The bedroom window was dug through with frost. Rupert had to blow on it and rub the wet, murky glass with the cloth over his wrist. The window began to clear: Rupert caught a naked woman through a patch of glass. Lady Marilyn. She was lying on a rumpled bed, with half her body out of the blanket. He had never seen a human creature in such repose. Isaac's little girl, without a dent on her face. Only the size of her breasts and the roundness of her nipples could have warned you she was fully grown. A crease appeared on her forehead. Marilyn scratched her nose, and the crease was gone.

Rupert was in misery. Those bosoms reminded him of Esther. She had the same spill on her chest, a soft swell under her arms. Rupert was no connoisseur of a woman's fleshy parts. Esther had been his only girlfriend, first and last. But Marilyn's tits made him cry. They could turn a boy gentle if he didn't have an irrevocable mission, and bile in his heart from Essex Street. He would have to murder her with his eyes closed.

Marilyn had been dreaming, not of Blue Eyes, not of Isaac, not of her mother Kathleen, but of Larry, her first husband, the one Isaac hadn't picked. He wasn't respectable enough for the daughter of a police chief; Larry had no permanent occupation. He fingered his guitar for a macrobiotic restaurant, sold scarves in the street. Isaac didn't chase Larry out of Manhattan; it was Marilyn's own gruffness, inherited from Isaac and Kathleen, the hysteria of an Irish-Jewish child, that got him to pack the guitar and leave. She was too wild for her men. Her devotion came with claws. She'd wanted to scratch the air around Larry to protect him from her father. But Larry disappeared. She didn't have to scratch for Coen's sake. Blue Eyes had a holster and a gun.

She heard a squeak from the window. Something pushed against the glass. The window chains were rattling. Marilyn could see a line of snow. There was a face in her window, a face with a bloody eye and a sinister nose. She didn't scream for Coen. She watched the hunching boy, one leg on the fire escape, the other leg in her father's room. He wore sneakers in a storm, and a crazy police coat. "Don't be shy, Mr. Snow Pants, come on in," Marilyn said, with the blanket still in her lap. She wasn't going to curtain herself for a boy in the window.

Blue Eyes came out of the bathtub after Marilyn's call (he'd been soaking off the wine Marilyn had poured on him). Blood in an eye couldn't throw him off: he recognized Philip's boy from the circulars Isaac's men had prepared. But he couldn't understand what Rupert was doing with a spoon in his fist. Coen was undressed. He could feel a chill on his balls. Rupert climbed out the window. Coen grabbed for his pants and shirt. He didn't have time to lace his shoes. Marilyn pulled on his shirttails. "Manfred, what the fuck is going on?"

Blue Eyes left his gun in the bathroom; he wasn't going to duel with a fifteen-year-old bandit. He had to shove Marilyn's hand off his back. "It's your father's war," he said. He was out on the fire escape before Marilyn could find another hold on his body. The wind blasted under his shirt. "Jesus," Coen said. The fire escape was dipping like a boat. He felt certain it would break from the wall and crash into the street. He followed Rupert up the ladder. It wasn't recklessness in Coen. Nothing could chase him off the fire escape. He had to take little Rupert.

"Blue Eyes," Rupert muttered on the ladder. He should have figured Isaac's sweetheart would spoil it for him. He grew careless about the rungs, leaping crookedly with a squeeze of his hands and a rapid kick. He was aiming for the roof. His foot got caught in the ladder, his sloppy left sneaker wedging under the side bar, between two rungs. "Goddamn," he said, trying to work his heel out of the sneaker.

The ladder rocked under the weight of Coen and the boy. Blue Eyes had to hug the ladder with both arms to keep his balance. He went up with the crawling motions of a baby. He pushed snow off his eyebrows, so he could watch Rupert's struggles with the ladder. "Rupert, wait for me." The snow smothered his voice.

Rupert's heel came free. He abandoned the trapped sneaker and started to climb again. He couldn't grip a ladder with a naked foot. It slipped off. Clutching with his hand, he missed the rung over his head. He had air and snow in his fingers. He fell. He didn't shape screams with his lips. No phantasmagoria pursued him as his body whirled. He didn't have flashes of Esther, Marilyn, or Isaac. He remembered nothing but his father's face. The squeezed-up skin with forty years of hurt. His mouth puffed open. He was trying to say dad.

Blue Eyes couldn't break Rupert's fall. The boy plunged in

widening arcs outside Coen's reach. It was a dangerous wish: Coen didn't have steel pinchers to fetch a diving boy. Rupert's body would have ripped him off the ladder. Coen felt that smack into the snowbank with the hollows of his eyes. The shivers came down to his jaw. Was he crazy? Or had the boy begun to move? A hand pushed out from under a pile of snow. Rupert wasn't dead.

16.

———

The woman with the suitcase was muttering in the hall. Doctors and nurses jumped out of her way. "Blue Eyes," she said; Marilyn had invaded Bellevue. She climbed up to the prisoners' ward and screamed at the metal door. "Manfred, come on out." The watchman thought she was insane.

"That's police business, young lady. You can't go in there."

"I am the police," Marilyn said.

The watchman grumbled to himself about the retards who were running loose on his floor. His name was Fred. "Yeah, you're a cop, I'm a cop, and the junkies in this ward wear badges on their pajamas."

"My father's a commissioner," she said. "Now open up."

"Lady, do me a favor. Disappear. You know how we get rid of pests? We stuff them in the laundry chute."

"Scumbag," Marilyn said, in her father's voice. "Did you ever meet Isaac the Pure?"

The watchman began to doubt himself. "What about Isaac?"

"I'm the only daughter he has. You understand? Bring me Blue Eyes."

"Blue Eyes? Why didn't you say you wanted him?" The watchman paged Manfred on the house telephone. Marilyn heard the click of an electric lock, and Blue Eyes came through the door. The watchman stared at the two of them; they had the same miserable look: runny noses and raw, scratchy eyes. Lovebirds, the watchman suspected. Goddamn lovebirds.

Coen picked up Marilyn's suitcase and spoke to the watchman. "Mind the store, Freddy. I'll be right back." Then he took Marilyn over to a closet behind the elevator shafts. He didn't say a word about the suitcase.

"They'll strangle me if anybody catches you up here."

"How are they going to manage that? You're the man with the gun. . . . Manfred, come with me."

"I'm supposed to be guarding Stanley Chin. Isaac rings every half hour. He still thinks Cowboy intends to swipe the kid."

"Manfred, are you deaf? I'm splitting, and I want you to come."

"Marilyn, I'm a city boy," Coen said, groping with his tongue. "I wouldn't dig weekends in New Rochelle."

"Jesus," she said, "don't play stupid with me. Rupert is lying downstairs with a broken back. He nearly got himself killed on account of Isaac."

"What was he doing in your window? You don't climb fire escapes in a blizzard without an excuse. He was reaching for you."

"Sure he was reaching. With a spoon."

"Marilyn, he didn't come over to crack hard-boiled eggs. Not him. You can rip a person's throat off with less than a spoon." Coen touched the metal corners of the suitcase. "Where you going?"

"As far as I can get. Seattle maybe. Vancouver. Manfred, do I have to beg? He'll make you kill somebody, that father of mine. Or get you killed. It's all the same to him."

Coen shrugged. He had a dent in his cheek. "I aint so hot at running away. What could I do in Seattle? I'd miss the cockroaches. I'd go woolly without the street."

She could have grabbed him by the nose and led him out of Bellevue, but she sensed the futility of that. He couldn't abandon her father's fort. He was the blue-eyed "angel" of Isaac's squad. She stood on her toes to kiss him, caressing the blond hairs on his neck with her tongue flicking in his mouth. She didn't give him the chance to return the kiss, or squeeze her into the closet. She pulled the suitcase away from him and ran down the hall. She wasn't a girl who could tolerate slow goodbyes.

Coen listened for the clump of her shoes. He was afraid to watch. A bouncing suitcase would have fucked him in the head. He loved that skinny girl. But the blizzard had stopped, and they couldn't hide in Isaac's blanket, or crawl to Seattle. How could he walk away from Isaac with Isaac's girl in his fist?

❖

The Chief had communed with his spies: two petty gamblers from Ninety-second Street swore on their mothers' holy graves that Zorro Guzmann would be coming down to the Port Authority terminal to collect a load of runaway girls arriving on a bus from Memphis. Isaac was suspicious of gamblers who took to swearing on a grave, but he couldn't snub the opportunity of catching Zorro with twelve- and thirteen-year-old bait. So he crouched on a platform over the big clock with four faces, where he could pick out Bronx pimps and Tennessee girls sneaking along the main concourse of the terminal.

He kept his chin behind an early edition of *The New York Times,* with a police radio tucked under his belt. The radio allowed Isaac to confer with his "angels," who skulked through different parts of the terminal, some of them in women's clothes.

"Isaac, we'll grab the Guzmanns with their pants down, you'll see," said Newgate, the FBI man. He had come along with Isaac as a neutral observer, trying to steal the First Deputy men's techniques. He wore wraparound sunglasses in late February, with a piece of Isaac's newspaper against his mouth. He had the grubby feel of a white slaver.

The radio ticked in Isaac's belt. One of his "angels" was summoning him from the Greyhound baggage room near the Ninth Avenue exit. "Isaac, it's going down. The two gloms are here. Zorro and his brother."

"Not so loud," Isaac muttered into his belt.

"Chief, should we piss on their earmuffs?"

"No. Stay where you are."

Zorro and Jorge Guzmann strolled onto the main concourse in wool sweaters and balding earmuffs, tracked by

Isaac's "angels." Zorro came without his checkered coat, or his pigskin shoes. Earmuffs must have been his uniform in Manhattan. Newgate tittered at the Chief. "Remember, Isaac, if they touch one little girl coming off a bus, they belong to me."

Jorge stood under the big clock while his brother went into a telephone booth. Newgate sucked his fingers. Zorro came out, and the Guzmanns continued their stroll. They didn't look at the platform over their heads. They ignored the "angels" on the escalators, and the weird women with walkie-talkies in their shopping bags. They didn't smile, or tinker with an earmuff. They left the terminal without a boodle of Tennessee girls.

Newgate sulked. "Isaac, how did they make us? Who gave them the word?"

Isaac rushed down to the telephones east of the clock. He found a slip of paper in Zorro's booth. It read, "Eat me, Isaac." He sent his "angels" back to Headquarters. He had to duck the FBI man now. "Newgate, I'm going to see my mother. So long."

He rode crosstown in a taxi, stopping the cab a block from Bellevue, near the old medical college. He paid the driver, got out, and lunged at a girl. Her suitcase spilled open. Marilyn began picking underpants off the street. Isaac wouldn't help.

"You don't have to worry, papa. I'm not going to bother Manfred any more. He's yours. God, you get loyalty from your slaves. He had the choice. Blue Eyes wouldn't budge. Isaac, you must be the greatest lay in New York."

Marilyn crept over the underpants. Isaac had to lift her off the ground. Holding her, he could feel his shame. He had manipulated Marilyn and Coen, tricked them into coming

233

together with Rupert on the prowl. Still, her jabber didn't make sense. He pulled Coen once Rupert dove under Marilyn's window, but that didn't qualify him as a "great lay," or anything else. Isaac wasn't pimping for Manfred Coen. He slapped at the suitcase, with garter belts and shirt sleeves dangling from the bottom. "Where the hell are you taking that?"

"To Far Rockaway," she said.

"Don't get cute with your father. I'll march you right home. I'll strap you to Rivington Street."

"I know," she said. "You'll roll blintzes for me and Ida."

She ran towards the medical college, hugging the suitcase with one arm. Isaac couldn't smile at the feeble pumping of her knees. His own skinny daughter was trying to escape from him, running to a college for protection. He had to yank her by the hair before her knees would slow down. "Crazy bitch, you think you'll get asylum in there? You'll ask mercy from a bunch of imbeciles who've been looking at corpses all day. They'll wheel you to the morgue with a lump of sugar in your mouth, those ghouls."

Her eyes were bulging from the knuckles in her scalp, and Isaac let her go. She had that mad concentrated scowl of her mother; Kathleen was the single person in this world who could frighten him. Mother and daughter, they knew how to squeeze the flesh under a man's heart. "Baby," he said, "what's wrong?"

His purring had no effect. She was shaking under her coat. Burrs appeared in her forehead, long burrs that could split a girl's brain. Isaac launched her with a soft shove. "You're free," he said. She didn't move. With two fingers he quieted the burrs in her head. She trudged towards Second Avenue, losing a sock on the way. Isaac recognized the queerness of that sock. Magenta wasn't Marilyn's color. The sock belonged to Coen.

Isaac crossed over to the hospital. He walked under the hump of a glass canopy that was shedding layers of ice. He entered Bellevue with two wet ears. Isaac couldn't afford to bully the girl at the main desk. Police chiefs weren't allowed near Rupert's bed without a pass. Rupert was in the custody of Manhattan children's court; Isaac had to keep his fingers off a fifteen-year-old boy. He mumbled "Rupert Weil" to the girl at the desk.

The girl said, "Sorry. You can't go up. His pass box is empty. He has visitors in his room."

Isaac drew out his badge. "Miss, I'm a friend of his father. A personal friend. Deputy Chief Inspector Sidel. Would I harm the boy? Ask your supervisors. I'm at Bellevue twice a week."

The girl stared at the blue and gold leaves on Isaac's badge. She scribbled a pass for him. "Fifteen minutes," she said. "That's all you're buying from me."

Isaac crouched upstairs. He showed his pass to a measly sheriff from the children's court who was guarding Rupert. Any quiff could have gotten past this sheriff. It was lucky for the children's court that Isaac had Stanley Chin, or the hospital would have lost Rupert and the sheriff's pants.

Isaac could see Rupert from the door. The bastards had mummified him; he was taped to a board, with a pulley near his feet. Only a piece of him remained unbandaged, a crooked oval from his eyebrows to the cleft under his lip, including most of his ears. His cheeks had turned a hospital yellow.

There was nothing sickly about Rupert's eyes; they were

bearing into Isaac with the hunger of a boy who couldn't be trapped on an inclined board. Isaac had to look away; you could catch brain fever gaping at a boy who never blinked. His body caught in traction, unable to move, he would have finished Isaac with the hooking power in his eye. The Chief respected such intransigence. But he wasn't getting into a staring war with Rupert Weil. Isaac couldn't win.

He was hit with a maddening smell by the door; he noticed boxes of caramels, black halvah, lollipops with sharpened sticks sunk into them, colored sugar water in little wax bottles that you had to break with your teeth, swollen marshmallows, and white chocolate sitting on a chair. These items must have been transported from the Bronx, where the Guzmanns owned a candy store. Isaac howled at the sheriff, who was asleep.

"The visitors Rupert had, did they come with earmuffs on their stupid heads?"

The sheriff made a timid "yes" with a shake of his jaw. Isaac sprang into the corridor with a closed fist. Zorro had been in and out of the hospital before Isaac could scratch his nose. Jorge brought the lollipops and the Russian halvah. Isaac came with empty pockets. The Guzmanns were too primitive to destroy with the rough, grinding hours of orthodox police work. They could slip between spies and two-way radios, and make themselves invisible to undercover men in padded brassieres.

Muddling over the Guzmanns, Isaac crossed shoulders with Mordecai and Philip, and the three Jewish musketeers of Seward Park were reunited after a lapse of twenty-seven years. They were awkward with each other. Mordecai molded his cap between his knuckles. Philip pulled the webbing under his hand-painted tie. Isaac brushed the radio in his belt with a fingernail. Mordecai, who was always in the middle, a trifle less severe than the two geniuses, spoke first.

"Isaac, a detective should know something about the human body. The doctors tell us stories about a severed nerve. Do you think Rupert will ever talk again?"

"Mordecai," Philip said, "is Isaac a magician? How can he predict?"

"Philip, don't cheapen his talents. Isaac is a master at predictions. Didn't he predict where my daughter was? He took Honey out of the gutter . . . only that was a month ago. And he gave your son back to you. What does it matter that Rupert will have to walk with three canes? He's alive."

"Mordecai," Philip said, "that's enough."

Isaac's puckered belly itched inside his slipover. Could he play the Chief with old friends? "Philip, I'm sorry. It was a crazy accident. I swear to you, my detective didn't throw him off the fire escape."

Mordecai sniggered in Isaac's face. "Coen? That guy couldn't push a baby into a puddle. Isaac, your hand was behind the whole thing. You gave the push from your lousy Headquarters."

Philip said, "Shut up."

"Why? Didn't he have Rupert's face on his posters? They would have shot him in the street like a dog. Isaac, I don't forgive what Rupert did to Sophie and the other people. But there's a difference between a demented boy and a cop with dirt in his ears."

Philip dragged Mordecai by his arm. "Isaac, we have to

go." They shuffled down the corridor, closing in on the sheriff and Rupert's ward, Mordecai struggling against Philip. Isaac had to shout. "Philip, I'll call you . . . tomorrow."

Isaac's shoes dug into Bellevue linoleum. He could march downstairs to his mother, or up one flight to Coen. The cuff of his trouser leg swished into the wall as Isaac selected Blue Eyes and the prisoners' ward. He'd sit with Sophie in the afternoon. He needed Coen's smile.

The watchman upstairs saluted Isaac. Freddy was in awe of the Chief. "Isaac, do you have a daughter with light brown hair? She was shouting high and low, but I couldn't let her in. That's the rules."

Even on a day shattered by the Guzmanns and Mordecai, Isaac had enough pluck to soothe a watchman. "Fred, you did right."

Freddy clicked the lock for him, and Isaac went inside. The prisoners' room was bombed out. Isaac had stepped into a war zone. The beds were scattered in a wretched design that made no sense. A junkie lay under one of them, huddling with a child's top that was much too feeble to spin for very long. The walls had large seams in them, and fresh bites; Isaac could have gone into the plaster with his elbow. Coen was with Stanley Chin.

They didn't have any greetings for Isaac. They stared at him from Stanley's hospital crib, adrift in their own shallow sleep. Isaac had the urge to blow dust out of their eyes. "Manfred, what's happening?"

Finally Coen smiled. Isaac expected more. Manfred's cheeks were too tight. Isaac understood the source of it: the boy had Marilyn on his mind.

"Isaac, should I send out for cupcakes and tea?"

"No cupcakes," Isaac said. "Where's the checkerboard?"

"We only got chess players in here," Stanley hissed at the Chief.

Isaac frowned. Pushing pawns with Coen could remind him of fire escapes and a certain black bishop. He noticed the warped ping-pong table, and the yellow balls. He wanted to challenge Blue Eyes in front of Stanley Chin, take Coen at Coen's game. But the two sleepy faces near the crib unsettled him. Isaac grew timid. He didn't reach for the yellow balls.

❖

The Chief had a gift waiting for him at Centre Street: a special edition of *The Toad*. Isaac's mug was on the cover, with the word "ASSASSIN" in boldface and the by-line of Tony Brill. Brodsky and the rubber-gun squad couldn't hide the covers from Isaac. Barney's men swarmed through Headquarters, from the basement to the giant cupola over the PC's rooms, stuffing *The Toad* into every available corner.

"Garbage," Brodsky announced, after reading Tony Brill. *The Toad* accused Isaac, in wavering margins and blotchy ink, of mounting a "death campaign" against Rupert Weil and the children of New York. "Who's next?" Tony Brill screamed from the second page. "How many of us will have to give up our sons and daughters to the Behemoth at Police Headquarters? Will we all land inside the Blue Whale?"

"Pure shit," Brodsky told the Chief. "Isaac, should I break his feet?" The chauffeur realized the absurdity of his threat.

Tony Brill was unapproachable now. The rumor at Headquarters was that Brill had jumped from *The Toad* to *Time*
magazine.

"Brodsky," Isaac said, "go scratch yourself. I'm busy." He
made Brodsky close the door. The Chief had something to do.
If he concentrated on the Guzmanns, he wouldn't have to
think about Marilyn the Wild. So he planned his next as-
sault. The Guzmanns were immune to First Deputy snares.
Jorge had forks in his earmuffs that could sniff a handgun out
of girdles and brassieres. Isaac wouldn't use ordinary spies.
He'd have to place a cop in deep, deep undercover. Who
would go into the Bronx to poison the Guzmanns' black
halvah? Brodsky? Coen? Cowboy Rosenblatt? Isaac was in a
fix. He had nobody to send. Marilyn crept into that country
between Isaac's walls. He couldn't fish her out of the room.

The rubber-gun squad stood with their chins near Isaac's
door. They were cursing Tony Brill and tearing Isaac's picture
off the covers of *The Toad*. "Shhh," Brodsky said. "You want
to disturb the boss? He's thinking in there."

Marilyn the Wild had gone to Port Authority. She sat by
herself on the uppermost deck of the terminal, hunched
against her suitcase. She had hours to kill before the next
crosscountry bus. She roosted a quarter of a mile from the
escalators, in an isolated spot. The prospect of company, male
or female, could make her nauseous. She'd spill her guts on
the wall if she had to explain her flight from three husbands,
blintzes, and her father. She didn't want to say "Isaac."

A dude in vinyl buckskin spotted Marilyn on his fourth stroll through the terminal. This dude went by the name of Henry. The sweep of Marilyn's stockings couldn't turn him on. Henry was interested in her suitcase. He'd swiped a Polaroid in the morning, and a silk umbrella; with Marilyn's stuff, he could visit his Jew on Thirty-seventh Street and collect a twenty. He'd fallen in love with a hat in Ohrbach's window.

"Hiya, sweet potato," he said, sitting down next to the suitcase. Marilyn's scowls couldn't pull him away. Henry wondered if the girl was a "pros." Who else would rest on a balcony with one foot off the ground? Only a whore. She had adorable knees, a strong Irish face, with bumps under her coat where her tits ought to be. Somebody owns this broad. Suppose it was Zorro, the Bronx spic, who had pimping rights at every bus station in New York. Henry could get his ears chopped off. The Guzmanns weren't human. They came from a forest in Peru. If you tampered with their women, they would bite your nose and leave parts of you in a paper bag. It was a risk Henry had to take.

First he'd explore a little. "Are you a friend of Zorro, sweetheart?" The whore wouldn't answer him. "Are you Guzmann merchandise?" Henry felt safer now. He snatched the suitcase, shouting, "See you, baby," and ran for the stairs, because the fucking escalators were too far away.

Marilyn stayed on the bench without crying "Thief." She wasn't so attached to a pile of underpants. She'd get another pair when the bus stopped in Chicago. Unencumbered, she could travel with a toothbrush in her pocket. She began to doze.

Dreaming, she saw a buckskin suit, a thief with dangling legs. She didn't have to touch her cheeks. The suitcase was near her toes. A man was lugging Henry by the nape of his fake buckskin collar. Blue Eyes. She could have strangled him with affection if that thief hadn't been around. She was dying to lick behind his ears.

Coen was sheepish with her. "Marilyn, I snuck out of Bellevue. I have forty minutes. Stanley is covering for me. I figured you'd be here. But I wouldn't have gotten to you without this glom. I noticed what he was carrying."

"Manfred, there's a million suitcases like mine."

"That's true. But how many of them have purple underpants sticking out of the side?"

They laughed, while Henry had a crick in his neck. He assumed Coen was a gorilla who worked for Zorro. He stuck his fingers in his chest and prayed. He'd heard that in spite of Peru the Guzmanns were religious people. Would they send a priest for him before they peeled his face?

"Marilyn, should I let him go? He led me to you, didn't he? And if I pinch him, we won't have any time for ourselves."

Marilyn wasn't greedy. She kissed Henry on the forehead and thanked him for bringing Coen. Henry creased his lips into a quarter smile. Then he galloped towards the escalators. After Coen he couldn't trust the stairs.

Marilyn fumbled with Blue Eyes, her arms inside his camel's hair coat, her teeth knocking into his jaw. The cop didn't resist. He had most of her blouse in his hand. Marilyn kicked off her shoes and wiggled out of her skirt. She would have pulled Coen down on the bench with her, but the cop became suspicious. "Marilyn, there are Port Authority detectives running around. They could snitch on us to Isaac."

"Who cares about snitchers?"

Coen spied an alcove about twenty feet behind Marilyn.

It was the entrance to an abandoned toilet. He picked up skirt, blouse, and suitcase. Marilyn carried her shoes. The alcove was narrow, and they had nowhere to lie down. Marilyn leaned into a dirty wall. Coen's pants dropped to his knees. Their bellies met under the coats. "Blue Eyes," she said. Soon her mumbling was indistinct.

❖

Taped to a moveable bedboard, a hospital boat with wheels, Rupert stared up at his father and Mordecai, the two shabby princes of Essex Street. He couldn't say papa, or mouth welcomes to Mordecai. Falling off Isaac's fire escape, he'd landed on his neck and lost the power of speech. He wasn't dumb to his father's words. Only Mordecai kept interrupting Philip.

"Rupert, listen to us. No cocksucker cop can get into your room again. There's a guard outside with a gun. If that's not enough, me and your father will sit with you. We'll stop Isaac next time. Rupert, you want some orange juice? Just wiggle your chin."

Rupert's chin was encased in thick swads of gauze. A nurse had shaved his skull, and wrapped him in a hundred feet of bandage. He didn't have one free toe.

"Moron," Philip said. "How can he signal for juice?"

The princes began to bicker. A team of nurses drove them out of the room. Mordecai scratched his knee. Rupert watched the hunched lines of his father's back. Candy stripes on a twenty-dollar shirt couldn't hide the bumps under Philip's shoulder blade. Rupert screamed inside his head. So long, papa. So long, Mordecai. He'd have to mother these two men. They had gray tufts behind the ears: neither of them was a grandfather yet. Mordecai walked with bent knees. Philip had a crooked neck from the years he'd given to crouching on Essex Street. Rupert would take his father out of Isaac's territories. They'd ride the currents on Third Avenue in Rupert's hospital boat. They'd settle in a different part of the borough (Philip would die without a few yards of Manhattan). They'd send for Mordecai. The three of them would make war on the pimps who were holding Honey. Then Rupert would bounce upstairs on his bedboard and pluck Stanley Chin out of the prisoners' ward. The cops would scream for the big Jew. Rupert wouldn't care. Isaac didn't exist above Delancey Street.

Rupert's bliss began to fail. How could he pull Esther out of the ground? Clay in her ears wouldn't bring her alive. His groin was shrewder than miles of bandage. Bellevue, Isaac, and the mummy's bag they'd wrapped him in couldn't stop his erection from pushing through the gauze. He was crying without a pinch of water in his eyes. These weren't a mourner's brittle tears. His hunger for Esther Rose couldn't be quieted with a doctor's needle, or sugar in his veins.

From time to time an intern would appear and marvel at the broken boy and his erection. The boy's nurses could see the swelling in the gauze. They giggled among themselves. "Practically unconscious and he gets it up." Rupert would growl at them behind immobile cheeks. Where's Mordecai? Where's my dad? And when they flipped him over, spanked his thighs to lessen the possibility of bed sores, Rupert would hiss through his nose. Ladies, you can't kill a lollipop.

The door opened. He expected orderlies in filthy green coats to change the tubes and pans under his bed. He saw mittens in a wheelchair and a sad-faced cop. It was Blue Eyes and Stanley Chin. Rupert smiled without untightening his lips. The cop was reticent. He wouldn't approach the bedboard. "Tell him," Stanley pleaded. "Can't you tell him?"

Coen dangled an arm behind the wheelchair. "Didn't mean to chase you in the storm . . . you shouldn't have climbed for the roof . . . the Chief's got a tricky fire escape. Rupert, I'm sorry."

The cop was silent again. Rupert didn't have to look very hard. The storm wasn't over for Blue Eyes; flecks of color exploded around Coen's enormous pupils. Where's Lady Marilyn? Coen was as sad as Mordecai. Mummified, stuck to a bedboard, he was glad he hadn't spooned blood out of Marilyn's neck. Coen could use her kisses.

"Rupe," Stanley said, grazing the mummy with plaster on his fist. "The bulls can't keep us apart. Shit, Mr. Coen snuck me down here. I'm not supposed to have visiting rights."

Rupert laughed underneath the canals of his nose. He could no longer feel the distant points of his body. He existed without fingers, elbows, or the blades of his knees. He had eyes, ears, and a sensitive prick. He couldn't laugh with his kneecaps, or get his belly to shake. His tongue lay dead. But he was grateful to Blue Eyes for bringing Stanley. He'd roll tongues in the back of his head. Clap out a dozen words. Stanley, we'll mend together. We'll grow new hands. We'll flood Bellevue with Isaac's songs.

The boys couldn't scrape their bandages in private. Nurses charged into the room. They had swollen red skin. "What do you mean, Detective Coen? Rupert Weil can't have any guests. Take your prisoner upstairs."

He heard the rattle of handlebars, the grunt of wheels, and he was in a world without Blue Eyes and Stanley Chin. The nurses grabbed his bedboard. They rotated him between their elbows, so Rupert couldn't fall. His erection was gone. His cheeks wobbled against the gauze. He was beginning to feel his knees again. The nurses put him back. "Rest," they said, as they hustled away from him. They screamed at the guard who had been assigned to Rupert by the children's court. "No one gets through this door. Not even the Chief of Police."

Rupert dreamed with an eye on the wall. There were shouts and sputters in the corridor. He saw patches of Philip and Mordecai. The two princes from Essex Street were arguing with nurses, doctors, orderlies, and Rupert's guard. "Are you crazy?" Mordecai said. "This is the boy's father. We want some satisfaction, please. We'll crush your lungs if we can't get in." A hole formed in the wedge of nurses' uniforms. The princes slipped through. They arrived at the bedboard. Rupert didn't have the capacity to wink at them. Papa, he said. Papa and Mordecai.